A Mystery of the Big Woods

by G. H. Teed

First published in *The Union Jack Library*,
No. 997, 18 November 1922.

Illustrated by E. Simmonds

Stillwoods Edition, 2019

Stillwoods.Blogspot.Ca

A MYSTERY of the BIG WOODS.

Illustrated by : :
E. SIMMONDS.

Introducing SEXTON BLAKE, Detective, and his assistant, TINKER.

This grand yarn, written by the gifted creator of Mademoiselle Yvonne and Dr. Huxton Rymer, is one you will really enjoy. The scene of the story is laid in New Brunswick, Canada, in which place the author was born and which he knows intimately. This, and the atmosphere of mystery and detective work which he can convey so well, make exceptionally good reading

THE FIRST CHAPTER.

Two Weary Travellers — The Big Woods — Stephen Hamilton — Startling News — Who Shot Angus Carson ? — Complications.

"AROOSTOOK JUNCTION! 'Roostook 'tion! Change here for Plaster Rock!"

As the brakeman's raucous voice shrieked out the information, and the door at the end of the antiquated railway carriage slammed, two passengers, who occupied one of the iron-framed, red plush double seats half-way down the car, reached for their hats, and began to gather their bags together.

"Not much more to go now, Tinker," remarked the elder of the two, as he stuffed some magazines into his bag and closed it. "If the Plaster Rock train is on time, we will be there in time for the evening meal."

"And a good job, too, guv'nor!" grunted the youngster, as he heaved a big suitcase into the aisle. "New Brunswick may be a darned fine province, but these trains up here in the woods don't try to break any speed records."

Sexton Blake smiled tolerantly, for he could quite understand Tinker's impatience at the leisurely manner in which the train had taken its way up the St. John River Valley on its way to the northern part of the province.

They had left St. John, the metropolis and chief port of the province, early that morning, and the first part of the journey had been run at a speed sufficient to suit even Tinker.

But after about eighty miles they had had to change from the St. John-Montreal express into the slower train that ran from McAdam Junction up to the St. John River Valley through Woodstock to the big timber country of the north, where it would finally rattle into the terminus at Edmundston on the Quebec border.

U. J.—No. 997.

Catalogue Information:
Title: A Mystery in the Big Woods
Author: G. H. (Hamilton) Teed (1886-1938)
First Published: The Union Jack Library, No. 997, 18 November 1922.
Illustrated by: E. Simmonds
This Edition: Stillwoods, 2019.
ISBN Canada: 978-1-988304-61-8
Blog: Stillwoods.Blogspot.Ca
Author Blog: GHTeed.Blogspot.Com
Storefront: http://www.lulu.com/spotlight/lulubook22

Introducing SEXTON BLAKE, Detective, and his assistant, TINKER.

This grand yarn, written by the gifted creator of Mademoiselle Yvonne and Dr. Huxton Rymer, is one you will really enjoy. The scene of the story is laid in New Brunswick, Canada, in which place the author was born and which he knows intimately. This, and the atmosphere of mystery and detective work which he can convey so well, make exceptionally good reading.

[Digitized by Doug Frizzle for GHTeed.Blogspot.Com, January 2019.]

Originally most of the over 1000 'Sexton Blake' stories had no author listed. But there were many individuals in England that studied each story and eventually the editor/publishers relinquished and produced a list of most of the authors. G. H. Teed, born in New Brunswick, Canada, was described as the best of the bunch!

During his career he published over 400 stories, many of novel length, according to the chums at *fictionmags*.

This story is notable as being one of three, where the author returns to describe his home province of New Brunswick, Canada.

Doug Frizzle, January 2019.

THE FIRST CHAPTER.   Two Weary Travellers —The Big Woods —Stephen Hamilton —Startling News—Who Shot Angus Carson? —Complications.

"AROOSTOOK JUNCTION! 'Roostook 'tion! Change here for Plaster Rock!"

As the brakeman's raucous voice shrieked out the information, and the door at the end of the antiquated railway carriage slammed, two passengers, who occupied one of the iron-framed, red plush double seats half-way down the car, reached for their hats, and began to gather their bags together.

"Not much more to go now, Tinker," remarked the elder of the two, as he stuffed some magazines into his bag and closed it. "If the Plaster Rock train is on time, we will be there in time for the evening meal."

"And a good job, too, guv'nor!" grunted the youngster, as he heaved a big suitcase into the aisle. "New Brunswick may be a darned fine province, but these trains up here in the woods don't try to break any speed records."

Sexton Blake smiled tolerantly, for he could quite understand Tinker's impatience at the leisurely manner in which the train had taken its way up the St. John River Valley on its way to the northern part of the province.

They had left St. John, the metropolis and chief port of the province, early that morning, and the first part of the journey had been run at a speed sufficient to suit even Tinker.

But after about eighty miles they had had to change from the St. John-Montreal express into the slower train that ran from McAdam Junction up to the St. John River Valley through Woodstock to the big timber country of the north, where it would finally rattle into the terminus at Edmundston on the Quebec border.

It had been some years since Sexton Blake had been in the northern part of the province, and while Tinker had been in the southern part several times, he had never yet been in the Tobique country for which they were now bound.

It was to be a holiday jaunt, pure and simple, and each was looking forward keenly to the ten days or so which they would spend in the big forest, where a thousand different hues of russet and gold and yellow had come with October.

For the shooting season had come, too, and the moose were calling across the land of a hundred lakes; the caribou were trekking south from the wilds of Gaspe; the deer were springing through the twilit aisles of the forest; and the partridges were whining overhead.

It is not to be wondered that Tinker had cast many a longing eye at his two gun-cases as the train brought them deeper and deeper into the land of promise.

Before them lay the last leg of the railway journey. A short run up from Aroostook Junction to Plaster Rock where the big timber closed in on the railway, then along the short logging road to Black Water Lake, where the canoes waited, and so on through the chain of small lakes and streams, until they should reach the log-built lodge of their host, where it nestled among the spruce and fir at the edge of Caribou Lake.

They did not expect to see their host until they should reach Plaster Rock, for he had written to Blake in St. John advising him that he would wait with the horses and backboard at that place.

Therefore, it was with some surprise that they saw him as they descended at Aroostook Junction. But as he advanced swiftly to meet them, Blake noticed at once the absence of the usual genial smile.

His brow was puckered with on expression of worry quite alien to Stephen Hamilton.

The visit during the autumn to Hamilton's camp on Caribou Lake was the outcome of a promise made by Blake some time before.

There was nothing lacking in the cordiality of Hamilton's handshake, and his words of welcome were plainly sincere. In fact, he displayed an almost feverish satisfaction at the sight of Blake.

"So mighty glad you have come," he said, in his quick, clipped accents. "Aside from your visit, I am glad to see you for other reasons.

"But there is no time to explain now. Do you happen to know if there is a doctor on the train?"

Before Blake could reply, Hamilton caught sight of a man who was leaning out of the window of the rear carriage.

With a muttered excuse to Blake and Tinker, be dashed along, and they saw him talking earnestly to the man in the train.

Following that, the man's head disappeared, and a few seconds later he swung himself from the carriage, carrying a handbag in one hand.

As they came up Hamilton introduced the new arrival as "Dr. Taylor," and both Blake and Tinker remembered that he had boarded the train at Hartland.

"I was in luck to spot the doc," said Hamilton. "Dr. Taylor is on his way up to Grand Falls, where he practises.

"But I have persuaded him to come back to the camp with me. I will tell you all about it in the train as we go along. Now you three had better get aboard. I will join you in a few minutes. I want to send a telegram to Sheriff Maxwell[1] at Perth. He can start on to-morrow's train. Can't do anything more to-night."

With that, Hamilton hurried away, leaving his two guests and the medico whom he had dragged from the train completely at sea.

But they had no time then to puzzle over the matter, for the train for Plaster Rock was just about ready to pull out.

It was typical of all the branch-line trains in New Brunswick—just an antiquated engine with half a dozen freight cars behind it, and at the end two passenger coaches of the Canadian-American type that had been turned off the main express lines years before.

They were just a little more shabby than the one they had left. That was the only difference.

The rear coach was supposed to be for the accommodation of ladies, children, and men who did not smoke.

The next one, of the same style, its long aisle running the full length between the iron-framed, red plush-covered seats, with their reversible backs and a door at either end, were for the smokers, and generally the haunt of the rougher elements among the lumberjacks who fought shy of facing the other sex.

It was into this coach that Blake and Tinker dragged their stuff, and they had hardly got settled when the engine emitted a shrill blast, and began to pull out.

Leaning out, Blake caught sight of Stephen Hamilton racing for the train, and saw him swing aboard the rear platform of the last coach.

It was a close shave, but nothing out of the ordinary in those parts.

A few minutes later he opened the door of the second coach, and

---

1 Note.—The sheriff characterised in this story is purely fictitious, and is in no way meant to refer to any sheriff in New Brunswick. The present and past sheriffs of the district in which this story is laid have all been very efficient, very intelligent, and very courteous gentlemen:—The Author.

came towards them. He glanced round before he dropped into a place beside Blake; then he took out his cigar-case and passed it round.

"I guess you are all puzzled," he said, when the weeds had been lighted. "But I had so little time to do things, I couldn't explain before.

"First, though, doc, let me explain just who Mr. Blake is. He is the famous London criminologist of whom you have probably heard, and this young man is his almost equally famed assistant, Tinker."

Dr. Taylor looked alert and interested.

Blake had already come to the conclusion that although he was at present only a bush doctor, he possessed considerable ability that would have won him recognition in a much larger field.

"Why, of course I have heard of Mr. Sexton Blake!" he exclaimed. "I have even read some of Mr. Blake's monographs, principally those referring to his experiments on blood pressure and its relation to the nervous system, and the consequent causation of criminal suggestion.

"I am most awfully pleased to have had the opportunity of meeting you, Mr. Blake, and I hope we may have an opportunity to discuss some points about which I am keen to ask you."

Blake smiled deprecatingly.

"I am highly flattered, doctor," he said pleasantly. "I shall be very pleased to discuss any phase of the question with you.

"As my friend Hamilton seems to have no intention of breaking up the party at present, I have no doubt we shall find an opportunity."

"You will have plenty of chance out at the camp," put in Hamilton. "And now I will tell you what has happened, and explain why I dragged you off the train, doc.

"To begin with, have any of you ever heard of Angus Carson of Montreal?"

"Do you mean the head of the big flour-milling firm?" asked Blake.

"Yes; that is the man. He was an old friend of mine, and every year almost we went into the woods together for a few weeks, either down here in New Brunswick, up in Gaspe, or into the woods of northern Ontario.

"For the last few seasons we have come down here, and that is why I built the camp out on Caribou Lake.

"Well, we arrived here a week ago. There was no one else, as you, Blake and Tinker, were to complete the party.

"Too many would only spoil the moose and caribou hunting.

"Now, then, to get down to cases. To-day Carson and I had lunch at the usual time, and, as is often a habit of ours, at one end of the veranda.

"We had just finished, and I had left the table to get a box of cigars from the living-room when it happened. I wasn't gone more than two minutes at the very outside.

"When you see the camp you will then understand that at no time was I more than a few yards from where we had been sitting.

"In fact, through the open window of the living-room, I could see one corner of the table at which we had lunched.

"Well, sir, when I returned to the veranda I saw that Carson had fallen forward in his chair, his head and arms resting over his plate, while an apple which he had been peeling had dropped from his fingers and rolled across to where the whisky decanter stood.

"I thought he had had a seizure of some sort, and ran towards him. I got him by the shoulders, but almost at once I saw that he was dead.

"From that point, it did not take me long to discover that he had been shot—shot from behind, and the bullet had apparently drilled his heart clean."

Hamilton paused a moment, but no one asked any questions. They were too anxious to hear further details.

"There was no question in my mind but that it was foul murder," proceeded Hamilton. "In the first place, there wasn't either a rifle or a pistol on the veranda.

"They were all locked in the gun-cupboard in the living-room. Even so, there could be no question of suicide, disregarding the fact that he had been shot through the back, for Angus Carson was the last man in the world to think of such a thing.

"He was a fine old fellow, genial, upright, more than ordinarily well balanced, not a worry in the world, either financial or otherwise, and filled with a horror of anything like that.

"Nor could it have been an accident, for the only guns and pistols about the place were, as I have already said, locked up in the living-room.

"I left him just where he was, and after a look round, I took down the hunting horn we use for calling in the canoes from the lake, and blew a couple of blasts.

"That brought the men from the rear, four of them in all—the cook, a French-Canadian from up Green River way, the two French-Canadian guides whom I have employed for years, and a Japanese servant who had been with Carson for a very long time, and who looked after both of us in camp.

"That is the lot, and, while I didn't consider it likely that any of them could have been guilty of the deed, I questioned them closely.

"As I expected, they came clean, and each corroborates the story of the other, for all four had been in the shack at the rear having their midday meal when the shot must have been fired.

"They had all four been there when I sounded the hunting horn, and had been there for at least a quarter of an hour, whereas the whole thing had happened during the minute or so that it took me to enter the living-room and get the box of cigars.

"The next thing was to extend the inquiry to some person or persons unknown.

"Now, just hear with me a moment while I describe briefly how the camp is situated.

"It is built, as I have told you, Blake, after the log-cabin fashion, consists of four rooms all on the ground or only floor, with a veranda running round the whole building.

"It is built in a clearing close to the edge of the lake, the distance being only a matter of a score of feet or so.

"Off to the left, as one stands on the front veranda facing the lake, is a small clump of firs and pines which I left for ornamental purposes

"But otherwise, the clearing extends on each side to the edge of the primeval forest, say, a distance of thirty yards or so.

"Remember that from the time I founded the hunting horn and had questioned my men only a few minutes elapsed, and all the time I was watching the clearing.

"I feel pretty sure that no one crossed it during that short time, although, of course, I don't say it couldn't have been done.

"Where we had been sitting was at the end of the veranda in front of the cabin nearest to the clump of trees of which I have spoken.

"From the fact that Carson had been sitting with his back to that clump, and that the bullet had apparently come from that direction, I thought it possible that the murderer had been concealed there, and might still be there for all I knew.

"I have not said that what puzzled me more than anything else was the fact that I had not heard any sound of a report at the time.

"Nor had any of the men, and yet I know enough about guns to know that the shot which killed Angus Carson was fired at no great distance.

"On that conclusion, we made for the clump of trees, and combed it from one end to the other, but nary a sign did we find. We looked up into each tree as well, but there wasn't anyone concealed there.

"Following that, we extended our search to the shore of the lake. It is of soft sand, and any footprints would have been plainly outlined.

"We found plenty, but the guides soon proved that they were only of our own party, and I know that they could not be mistaken.

"Next we got out the glasses and scanned the lake in every direction. The only thing visible was a canoe at a distance of four miles or so.

"It was up near the head of the lake, and, of course, could not have made that distance under three or four times the period that had elapsed since the shooting.

"When we drew a blank there I sent one of the guides with the Jap and the cook to scour the woods.

"I took the other guide, and we started out in a canoe to search along the edge of the lake.

"We came back as ignorant as when we had started, and, later on, the other party came straggling in, having discovered nothing.

"I should say here that it rained quite heavily last night, and those guides of mine would have picked up any trail if it had been there.

"That is where I was forced to leave matters. We carried poor old Carson in, and laid him on his bed.

"Then I got into the canoe, and made record time to Black Water, where I got Napoleon St. Pierre to drive me into Plaster Rock in his buckboard. I just made the train as it was starting for Aroostook Junction. You know the rest.

"It is a complete mystery to me, and I can tell you I don't like it. Aside from the fact that I am keenly cut up over losing my old friend, I am deeply disturbed that it should happen at my camp when he was my guest, and when I was the only person present, or, rather, practically present, when it occurred.

"You may be able to discover something, doc, when you have

7

made an examination, and as for you, Blake—well, if you want a first-class mystery to unravel here is one ready made for you.

"If we can't discover who killed Angus Carson, there are bound to be some persons who will make nasty innuendoes about me."

"Nonsense!" said Blake emphatically. "It would be a most ridiculous suggestion.

"You could no more shoot a man in cold blood than could I or Dr. Taylor or Tinker."

"Of course I couldn't. But that doesn't go to say that others might think the same. Besides, there is something else about it that must be told to the proper authorities."

"What is that?" asked Blake quickly.

"This. Angus Carson was mixed up with me in one of my recent deals.

"He held my promissory-note for two hundred and fifty thousand dollars.

"When he came down to stay with me at the camp, I told him to bring that note along, as I would take it up while he was here.

"He did so, and I know that this fact must be known to his private secretary.

"I wrote to my bank in Woodstock the day of my arrival to realise on certain securities, and forward banknotes to me at Plaster Rock for the necessary sum.

"They arrived two days ago, and I paid them over to Carson. Carson gave me back the note, which I immediately burned.

"Then he handed me the money, and asked me to lock it away in a small safe I have at the camp until we should be going into Plaster Rock, when he could post it on to Montreal.

"That money is still in the safe under my care. But don't you see what might be inferred?"

Blake gave a low whistle.

"That certainly complicates matters." he said slowly. "But the fact remains that you could not shoot a man in cold blood, and, therefore, you are innocent.

"A further examination of the mystery may reveal the truth without much trouble. But whether it proves simple or difficult, you may take it from me, old friend, that I shall stick to the case until there is not the slightest chance of any suspecting what you fear!"

Stephen Hamilton shot out his hand, and the two men gripped.

"Thanks!" he said simply. "I can tell you I felt thankful when I remembered that you would be arriving to-day!

And well he might, for if any brain was capable of ferreting out the truth, it was that of the brilliant criminologist who sat beside him at that moment.

During Hamilton's absence Carson had fallen forward in his chair, his head and arms resting over his plate. He was quite dead—shot from behind.
(*Chapter* i.)

THE SECOND CHAPTER.   The Restigouche Country— Lumberjacks —Sweeney's Guide—Blake's Suspicions —A Wire to Lindsay.

A few years ago, when the writer of these lines passed through Plaster Rock, on his way up the Tobique River and on into the dense timber limits of the Restigouche country, the place consisted of some four or five houses, a small wooden frame hotel, which was used as a jumping-off place by the lumbermen on their way into the woods, and a general store, from which the different lumber-camps could draw supplies. These few buildings were scattered haphazard in rough clearings still dotted with stumps, close to the bank of the river, and it is probable that the place is practically the same to-day.

There may be one or two buildings more, or there may be one less, but whatever changes have occurred have been slight.

And close at hand the dark, brooding forest stands like a great wall, forbidding the further encroachment of civilisation.

It was dark when Stephen Hamilton and his party arrived, and, after handing over the baggage to the guide who had accompanied Hamilton from the camp, the four stumbled across the tracks, and made for two lighted windows, which revealed the whereabouts of the hotel—if such it might be called.

After several minor accidents they finally succeeded in reaching it, and as they mounted the high steps to the wooden veranda, which had been built on a spiderly pine foundation, fully twelve feet above the sloping bank that fell to the river, they saw half a dozen men seated in stiff wooden chairs, smoking or chewing, and muttering an occasional remark.

There was silence as Hamilton opened the door, allowing the light from within to fall on those behind him. Then two or three of the men—lumbermen, Blake could now see spoke to Hamilton, and, from their tones, Blake knew that the operator, for all his wealth, was well liked by the "white water" men.

The office of the hotel proved to be a small room, which was heated by a round iron stove, about which sat four more men.

Behind a tiny desk was a stout young woman, whose dark hair and eyes told of the blood of the voyageurs in her veins, and when she spoke this was confirmed by her marked accent.

It was that of the Canadian "habitant", which is heard throughout

Quebec province and in the northern part of New Brunswick, which is almost entirely French Canadian.

It was out of the question to think of driving out to Black Water that night, as the road was little more than a clearing through the woods in places, whilst in others it was of that particularly racking type known as "cordouroy," that was next to impossible to negotiate in the dark.

Therefore, they would have to put up with what accommodation the hotel could offer them for the night, and a very few minutes served to reveal the fact that they would have to double up, two in a room.

Blake and Tinker took one, while Stephen Hamilton and Dr. Taylor shared another.

The rooms were scarcely large enough for one person, let alone two, but in that country one learns to put up with inconveniences, and as all four were seasoned to hardships no one grumbled.

Then they descended to the little bare dining-room where the "habitant" girl, who seemed to be the general factotum of the place, had served supper.

A red tablecloth covered the square pine table, and on this was the usual collection of cheap glass and crockery, the plates and cups being thick and ponderous, for the lumberjack is not the man to whom one would give fragile china.

They were late, and, with the exception of one husky individual who sat at one end of the table, and whom they discovered later was gang-boss of the gang that was staying at the hotel, and was bound for the Restigouche timber limits to get the "tote" road laid out before the first snows should come, they had the place to themselves.

For obvious reasons, they said nothing about the tragedy that had taken place at the camp, but Blake made it his business to get into conversation with the gang-boss, and question him at considerable length about the country round about Caribou Lake, and whether he knew if many persons from the outside had gone through Plaster Rock recently.

But the gang-boss had not been near Caribou Lake since the previous spring, when he had come down the Tobique with the log drive, so Blake gleaned little.

After the meal, which was brief but wholesome, consisting of venison steak, potatoes, baked beans, thick slabs of white bread, and the inevitable chunk of pie—in this instance blueberry—they sauntered out to the veranda and seated themselves at one end of the crowd already gathered there.

Some of the lumberjacks now recognised Dr. Taylor and when Stephen Hamilton had started a conversation with one of them the talk became general.

No introductions were made, and, of course, the lumberjacks never dreamed that the somewhat silent man. who spoke with such crisp decision when he did give voice, and the young man, were two very famous persons.

But they soon gave their respectful attention to the stranger, for it was not long before they discovered that Blake knew as much about timber and forestry as the oldest among them.

As the gang was to start up the Tobique at daybreak the gathering broke up early, and when the last "Good-nights" had been said and the last bit of horseplay ended the little party of four was left to itself.

Then Blake began to question Stephen Hamilton in low tones regarding certain points that had occurred to him while he had been thinking over the affair in his mind.

"In going over your story, Hamilton, I find that there is little chance of making any real progress until we get to the camp.

"I shall want to make a very careful examination of the ground and a reconstruction of the crime before I endeavour to form a theory.

"But we might save some time now by getting one or two points more clearly fixed in my mind.

"For instance, I take it that we must, for the time being, accept your belief that none of the four men employed at the camp is guilty."

"I feel that it is out of the question that any of them could be."

"Yes, that certainly looks reasonable. It would be most difficult to imagine a motive for any one of the three French Canadians to commit the murder.

"What was their attitude towards Mr. Carson? Had he at any time had occasion to censure them?"

"None whatever. In the first place, they were my servants, and, of course, if he had had any occasion to complain of inattention or discourtesy, he would have come to me.

"But I know that they liked him very much. He was a most experienced woodsman and they respected him for that.

"Moreover, I have reason to believe that he was extremely

generous with them."

"Then his death would be a loss to them with no chance whatever of it benefiting them. I think you are right.

"Now, about the Jap? You said he had been with Mr. Carson for many years."

"Yes. I don't know exactly how long, but I should say ten or twelve at least, I don't think there is anything fishy there, Blake. He appeared very fond of his master."

"Quite so. At the same time, we must remember that the Jap is a deep animal, and we don't know what obscure motive might influence a man like the Jap servant to commit a crime.

"But with the evidence that he was with the others at the time it seems that we must eliminate him as well.

"That lets out your household, and therefore we must look beyond. From what my logging friend told me at the supper table I have discovered that yours is not the only camp on Caribou Lake."

"Oh, no! There is a fishing-camp at the lower end of the lake which belongs to a New York group of men.

"They only come here in the spring and early summer for the trout and salmon fishing.

"Then there is another camp almost directly across the lake from where mine stands. It belongs to a Montreal stockbroker.

"Then beyond Caribou on the Big Moosehorn, there are two more camps, but I don't know whether there is anyone at them now or not."

"H'm! This man who has the camp across from you—the stockbroker—is he in residence?"

"Yes. I haven't seen him, but the guides told me he had been there for a couple of weeks or so."

"Did either you or Mr. Carson know him."

"I don't know him, but Carson did, although not intimately, I believe, as he referred to him in just a casual manner, and, if I remember rightly, in a rather disparaging way.

"Called him a bucketshop shark, or something like that."

"Ah! What is the mans name?"

"Sweeney—first name Ralph, I believe."

"How far is it across the lake from the point where your camp is situated?"

"About eight miles."

"And the length of the lake."

"Twelve miles. My camp is near the upper end, about four miles from the top, that is, in the direction of the stream that connects Caribou with Big Moosehorn."

"Thanks! And now, Hamilton, in relating what had occurred I think you said the only sign of anyone being about was a man in a canoe which you saw through the glasses about four miles away."

"That is so. But we couldn't make out who it was."

"That means it might have been this man Sweeney or a guide?"

"Yes; or a timber cruiser. They often come and go by the Caribou and Big Moosehorn."

"In which direction was the canoe heading?"

"Well, it seemed to be making for the stream that links up the two lakes, but, of course, it might have been making for Sweeney's camp. It was going away from us."

"It doesn't seem likely that a canoe four miles away could have any connection with the murder, but we will bear it in mind, nevertheless. I think that is about all I want to know to-night.

"I shall wait until we get out to the camp before asking any further questions, as I do not want to get my mind confused.

"What about turning in as we are getting away so early?"

"A good idea!" answered Hamilton, with a yawn, and at that the party broke up.

The following morning they were away on the heels of the lumber-gang, and as the springy buck-board negotiated the stretches of "cordouroy," neither Blake nor Tinker was sorry that they had waited until daybreak to make the start.

Black Water Lake, where they would leave the backboard and take to the canoes, was the first patch of water in the long lake and stream portage that ranged away through the big timber from the Tobique.

There was a solitary cabin at the end of the road, occupied by Napoleon St. Pierre, an old guide and trapper who supported a family of sixteen by a combination of trapping, fishing, hunting, and the occasional fees he picked up from the men who had fishing-camps on Caribou and Big Moosehorn.

Owing to the size of the party, it was necessary to requisition a second canoe, and after some delay, in which Hamilton arranged for the old habitant to bring the sheriff from Black Water to Caribou as soon as he should arrive, they got away.

It was six miles of easy paddling across Black Water to the connecting stream which led to Caribou and they made it in good time, but there was a half-mile portage half-way through that delayed them some time, as the canoes and bags had to be shouldered and carried round the rapids.

But from that on it was easy enough, and they came out on to the broad bosom of Caribou at a good clip.

"That is my camp," called out Stephen Hamilton, "and that," pointing towards the right shore, "is about where Sweeney's camp is located."

Blake nodded, and from that on kept his gaze fixed on Hamilton's camp.

As they drew nearer he could make out the details of the place— the big square-built log house close to the shore of the lake, the cookhouse and men's quarters at the rear, and a little to the right as one approached from the lake, the clump of spruce and fir off to the right; then beyond, the unbroken wall of the forest.

Each item he impressed indelibly upon his mind, and then as the canoes at last nosed into the sand, he regarded the man who had come down to meet them. Hamilton intercepted his glance and said:

"This is the other guide, Blake." Then to the man he went on: "Everything all right, Louis?"

"Oui, boss. Wan man lak' see you."

"Who is it?" asked Hamilton, in surprise.

"Ver' big man mak' for cross de lac."

"You mean the man from the other camp over there?"

"Oui, boss."

Hamilton turned, but Blake who had overheard the words had already caught sight or a figure seated on the front veranda of the cabin, and, in fact, at that moment the man rose and came down the steps towards them.

It was just then, too, that Hamilton caught sight of a strange canoe drawn up beside the half-dozen that served his own camp, and crouching in the shade was a guide whom he had seen about Caribou and Big Moosehorn, but whom he had never employed.

"That is Sweeney," he said, in a low tone "I wonder what on earth brings him here?" Blake studied the approaching stranger. Louis had described him well as a "ver' big man," for he was a giant of fully six feet three and broad in proportion.

Clean-shaven, about forty, Blake reckoned, with a heavy jaw and a hard blue eye. Blake knew the type well.

As he reached them he bowed slightly and smiled at Hamilton.

"I suppose you are surprised at my presence here," be said. "I heard from my guide of the unfortunate accident here, and came across to see if I could be of any assistance.

"I have never had the pleasure of meeting you, Mr. Hamilton, but I have seen you in Montreal many times, and if I can do anything at all I hope you will permit me to do so.

"I was aghast at the news, but more so when I arrived here and found that it was Angus Carson—an old business friend. My name is Sweeney. Perhaps Carson has spoken of me."

Hamilton shook hands perfunctorily.

"It was very good of you to come across, Mr. Sweeney. But I am afraid that there is nothing you can do. Yes, Mr. Carson did say that he knew you.

"Let me introduce you to Mr. Sexton Blake, of London, Dr. Taylor, of Grand Falls, and this young man, who is Mr. Blake's assistant, Tinker."

They all shook hands, then Sweeney said: "Am I right in presuming that you are the Mr. Sexton Blake, the famous criminologist?"

"I am a criminologist," replied Blake.

"Yes." broke in Hamilton. "Mr. Blake was coming here on a visit, and I consider it extremely fortunate that he arrived at such a time."

"Er—" began Sweeney hesitatingly.

"I mean because he is going to investigate this affair. It was not an accident, Mr. Sweeney, it was foul murder!"

"Murder!" exclaimed Sweeney. "How can that be possible? Who would kill Angus Carson? I haven't questioned any of your servants, but I understood from my own guide that it was an accident."

Blake had tried to catch Hamilton's eye in time to prevent him from stating to this stranger in such positive tones that it was murder, because it was quite possible that as matters progressed Hamilton's own position might not be too easy, and Blake did not want any more complicating factors than possible.

But the words had been spoken; and so no good could be done

now by trying to brush them aside.

"Yes," he said quietly. "Mr. Hamilton feels convinced that Mr. Carson was murdered, and we shall start without delay to run the murderer to earth.

"But first, I think we ought to make an examination of the victim. What do you say, doctor?"

Dr. Taylor nodded, and the party moved towards the steps.

As they passed the canoes. Blake noticed that as Hamilton's two guides, Louis and Pierre, passed Sweeney's guide, they each shot an insulting epithet at the man, which gave Blake to understand that bad blood existed between them.

Just an incident, but one which he filed away, in his mind, for future consideration.

Angus Carson lay on the bed in his room just as he had been placed by Hamilton before his dash for Plaster Rock.

The Japanese valet had covered the body with a sheet, and as the doctor drew it down it was difficult to realise that the tranquil features before them were those of a dead man.

Angus Carson had died swiftly; without time to realise what had happened to him.

The doctor's examination was brief, and it soon disclosed that the cause of death had been a bullet which had passed into the body just under the left shoulder-blade, and not far from the spine.

He opined that it had probably cut through the left lung before striking the heart, and, on examining the front of the torso, he found a small hole where the bullet had come through.

They found it soon after where it had fallen down into the folds of the shirt, the doctor passed it to Blake, who dropped it into his pocket with merely a glance at it.

Presently Blake, Tinker, Sweeney, and Hamilton returned to the veranda, leaving Dr. Taylor and the Jap valet to prepare the body.

Hamilton got out the whisky and soda and served it himself, while they talked in low voices of what had happened.

Following that, Sweeney accepted Hamilton's invitation to remain at lunch. He repeated his expressions of deep regret at the affair, and repeatedly voiced his difficulty in believing that anyone could have murdered Angus Carson,

"Could it have been any of your men, Mr. Hamilton?" he asked.

Hamilton explained why that suspicion was not tenable, and then

Sweeney said:

"Surely there will be some explanation of it. Why, with just you two here on the veranda, why—" then he stopped suddenly as though a new thought had just come to him, He laughed shortly.

"It's a good thing you and Carson were good friends," he said, with a smile. "Otherwise, some nasty people might raise some idiotic suspicions."

Hamilton felt disturbed, and showed it. It was exactly what he himself had feared, and now that a stranger had put the thought into words, it loomed up at him as a very nasty position indeed.

But the tension was broken by Sexton Blake's cool tones.

"Mr. Hamilton is not the type of man to shoot another in the back, Mr. Sweeney. Only very ignorant or very evilly-disposed persons could think that of him. Mr. Hamilton has nothing to fear.

"It is true that Angus Carson was murdered; at least, there doesn't seem room for the shadow of a doubt. Therefore, there is a murderer abroad, and eventually we shall lay him by the heels."

"I certainly hope you succeed in doing so," responded Sweeney heartily. "And, as you say only fools could suspect Mr. Hamilton of such a deed. By the way, have you notified Carson's family and business associates in Montreal?"

Hamilton shook his head.

"Not yet. I shall do that after the sheriff has made his investigations. He will be here by to-morrow at the latest, and he may travel through from Plaster Rock to-night, now, gentlemen, let us have lunch."

As they sat down at the table, Blake asked Hamilton to point out exactly where Carson had been sitting when he was shot, and for his benefit. Hamilton enacted the whole scene, including how he had entered the living room to get the cigars, and how he had come out again to find Carson sprawled over the table.

Blake made no comment when he had finished, although the others seemed to expect him to do so.

But Tinker knew that his apparent lack of interest was no criterion. It was when Sexton Blake seemed most indifferent that he was most dangerous.

Nor was it until Ralph Sweeney had taken his departure, and his canoe was only a small speck far out on the lake, did Blake show his hand. When he did, he acted energetically enough.

Securing a telegraph-form from Hamilton, he sat down at the desk in the living-room and wrote out a message. With this in his hand he returned to the veranda.

"I want Tinker to return to Plaster Rock and send this telegram," he said, addressing Hamilton, "He could return with Napoleon St. Pierre's son this afternoon."

"Why, of course, Blake, whatever you say. But why send Tinker all the way back! I can send one of the guides in with it."

"No!" said Blake decisively. "This is of a very private nature; and, besides, it is in code. I want Tinker to take it."

It was arranged in this way, and less than half an hour later Tinker and Napoleon St. Pierre's son were driving the canoe back across Caribou with long, steady strokes. And, besides Blake, only Tinker knew that the code telegram he carried was to Lindsay, Blake's Montreal correspondent, instructing him to telegraph all the particulars he could gather about Ralph Sweeney.

When the canoe had disappeared from view, Blake set to work in earnest on his examination of the place.

But little did he guess what a startling discovery he was to make before he completed his work.

THE THIRD CHAPTER.   A Reconstruction—The Japanese Valet—What Does He Know?—The Guides Take Exercise—A Startling Discovery.

BLAKE began by having Stephen Hamilton reconstruct in detail the exact position which Angus Carson had been in when the assassin's bullet had found him.

Not that he had not taken careful note of the previous demonstration, but he had not applied any great degree of mental analysis at that time, due to his desire to postpone the real investigation when the hampering presence of Ralph Sweeney had been removed.

Hamilton assumed a position in the chair which Angus Carson had occupied; as nearly like that in which he had found the murdered man.

While he remained thus, Blake, with Dr. Taylor, moved behind him, and there the doctor demonstrated exactly where the bullet had entered, and what course it must have followed before it emerged on the other side of the body.

Blake made the physician illustrate this with the utmost care, and when he had finished, Blake moved round, dropped to his hands and knees, and crawled under the table until he was close to Hamilton's knees.

From that position he again followed with his mind's eye the course of the bullet, and then, moving a little to one side, he extended the line of flight, so to say, until by carrying it out and out, he found that it finally became obstructed by the clump of fir and spruce-trees which stood a little way off, and to which reference has already been made.

Now Blake got to his feet and walked to the edge of the veranda. He stood gazing thoughtfully towards the clump for some minutes, then he turned and indicated that Hamilton might rise.

"What do you make of it, Blake?" asked the latter, as he got to his feet.

"At present I am inclined to think that the bullet came from the direction of that clump of trees," answered Blake.

"But I told you that was the first place we searched," protested Hamilton. "If there had been anyone there we should have found him before he could possibly have reached the main timber."

20

"Perhaps so," agreed Blake. "I didn't say that the bullet was fired by someone standing in the concealment of that clump.

"I said that in my opinion it had come from that direction. If my conclusions are correct, and I base them on the course the bullet took after entering the body, then, by extending the course of flight, the line rises gradually until it becomes obstructed by the upper part of the trees in the clump."

"You mean it was fired from high up in one of the trees?"

"That is my tentative opinion."

"But we looked up in the trees as well as on the ground," said Hamilton. "If there had been anyone there we should have seen him for sure."

"That is exactly why, for the present, I say my opinion is purely tentative. I am puzzled on that very point. But we shall make a further examination of the grove presently.

"We will confine our first efforts to those trees nearest the house, for the bullet must have been unobstructed by branches to come with such certainty.

"The curious part is how, if there was someone concealed there, he could get away without leaving any tracks. Not even a monkey could reach either the main belt of timber or the lake without finding it necessary to cover a certain amount of ground."

"Well, there were no tracks. As I have already told you, we had rain the night before, and if there had been any tracks, Louis and Pierre would have found them. There are no cleverer guides or trackers in the woods than those two fellows."

Blake nodded his agreement.

"Would you mind summoning the whole four men here?" he asked. "I should like to interview them."

For answer Hamilton raised his voice, and when the Jap valet appeared, he instructed him to call the others.

A few moments later they came round the corner of the veranda. They lined up before their master, who gave them orders to answer as plainly as possible any questions Blake might put to them.

Blake took the cook first.

"Do you speak English? he asked. "If you prefer, I will speak to you in French."

"I spik Eengless, boss," answered the cook readily.

He was a stocky, well-built little woodsman, and certainly did not look as if he had it in him to shoot a man in the back.

But Blake realised that one never could tell.

"What is your name?" he went on.

"Jean Thibault, boss."

"Where were you when your masters guest was killed?"

"In ze cook'ouse."

"What were you doing?"

"'Aving ze food wiz ze odders."

"Did you hear the sound of a shot."

"Non—nozzings."

"Think well. Your master's guest was killed while you were in the cookhouse, it is only a short distance from here. The shot which killed Mr. Carson was fired at fairly close range—that is certain.

"Are you quite positive you heard nothing —not even a slight sound?"

"Non, m'sieu. I hear nozzings, and zat is ze troof. Me, I hear nozzings onteel M'sieu 'Amilton 'e blow ze 'orn."

"All right, Jean, that will do for now. You next, Louis." But Louis was able to give no more information than Jean had done.

Blake then turned to the Jap valet.

"What is your name?" he asked suddenly in Japanese.

The eyes of the Jap flickered momentarily in surprise at being addressed with ease and fluency in his own tongue, but he answered readily enough:

"Kamoto, sir."

"You are from the south. What part?"

"Nagoya, sir."

"Your family?"

"My honourable father, is a worker in ivory, sir."

"How long have you been with Mr. Carson as his valet?"

"Eleven years next spring, sir."

"Where were you when he was killed?"

"Taking food in the cookhouse with the others, sir."

"Did you hear the sound of a shot?"

"No. I heard nothing until the honourable gentleman sounded the horn."

"You are absolutely sure on that score?"

"Perfectly, sir."

"What were the relations between you and your master, Kamoto?"

The Jap's eyes flickered again, but without hesitation he answered:

"My honourable master was most benevolent, sir. During all the years I served him, not once did he address me in anger. He was my father and my mother. I would have died for him!" he added simply.

Blake studied the impassive face for some moments, asking himself if that yellow mask really hid the devotion which Kamoto claimed to have felt for his dead master, or did it but mask some subtle form of Oriental guilt?

He could not possibly tell, but he determined to study the Jap closely. Now he asked Kamoto a question which he had not put to the three French-Canadians.

"Have you any suspicion as to how your master met his fate?"

Again that slight flicker of the eyes, then again as readily came the answer:

"No, sir."

"You were in constant association with your master. Did he, to your knowledge, have any enemies who might do this thing?"

The irritating, baffling flicker came again. "I can point to no one, sir."

"What were your plans for the future before this happened?"

"On the completion of twelve years service, it was my intention to leave my honourable master and return to my own country."

"You have saved sufficient money?"

"My honourable master was very good to me," responded the Jap.

Blake gave it up.

"Very well, Kamoto, you may go." he said curtly in English.

The Jap bowed and slipped back into the house, while Stephen Hamilton said quickly:

"I didn't know you could speak that lingo, Blake. Did you get anything out of him?"

"About as much as I would have got out of a wooden statue," responded Blake with a shrug. "I feel convinced that he knows something about this affair, but whether he is keeping silent because his knowledge is a guilty one, or whether he was as deeply devoted to his dead master as he maintains, I can't tell yet.

"But Master Kamoto wants a little studying."

"Carson always swore by Kamoto," remarked Hamilton.

"And probably had reason to," said Blake. "Now, Hamilton, will you please instruct Louis and Pierre to go across to that clump of trees.

"If you will accompany them, I will call from here and tell you exactly where I wish them to begin climbing. The cook may as well go back to his cookhouse."

When Hamilton had done as Blake wished, Blake once more followed out the imaginary line of the bullet's flight. When he had fixed a point in the trees, he raised his arm and pointed towards it.

"Let one of them try that tree first," he called. "I will tell him when to stop."

Hamilton made a gesture in Pierre's direction and the guide worked his way in between the lower branches of a giant fir-tree.

Blake watched him closely while he climbed up and up until he was a good thirty feet above the ground. At that point Blake gave the signal to stop. Then he called:

"Tell him to have a good look round up there, Hamilton. If he finds nothing, let him go a little higher. If he still finds nothing, we will try another tree."

Hamilton passed the orders on to Pierre, who began working his way around the trunk of the tree. It was apparent even to Blake and Dr. Taylor, who stood on the veranda, that he had come upon nothing of importance, so Blake gave the signal for Louis to tackle a tree which stood behind the other, but a little to the left.

Louis was soon scrambling up nimbly, and kept on climbing until Blake gave the signal to stop. Then he followed exactly the same procedure which Pierre had gone through, apparently without the slightest result.

By now both Stephen Hamilton and Dr. Taylor were sure Blake was following some sort of a blind trail, but Blake had not the slightest intention of giving up so soon.

Under his directions, Pierre and Louis were sent up tree after tree which could possibly be brought within the compass of two imaginary boundary lines which Blake had set as the utmost limits to which the flight of the bullet could have extended. The guides themselves were getting a bit peevish at the continual climbing up and down, but under their masters eye they kept at it.

It was the ninth or tenth tree which it was Louis' turn to ascend that was to prove the wisdom of Blake's persistency Even he himself was beginning to think the experiment would yield nothing when, Louis had reached a height or about forty feet from the ground, they heard him give a great shout.

Like a flash Blake was off the veranda and racing for the clump of trees. He burst through until he stood just beneath where Louis was sitting on a whorl of the branches high up. Hamilton and Dr. Taylor were standing panting beside him.

"What is it?" called Blake sharply. "What have you found?"

"Ma foi, m'sieu!" came the excited voice of the guide. "It ees wan gun!

THE FOURTH CHAPTER.   The Rifle in the Tree—A Mysterious Happening—The Mahogany Box—Murdered by Wireless.

"DON'T touch it, Louis!" cautioned Blake. "I am coming up!"

With that he forced his way through the lower branches and started to climb.

The fir-tree is by no means as easy to climb as the ordinary spruce or the red pine, for the fir needles are much sharper than the soft, flat needles of the spruce, and the trunk and limbs are rough.

But Blake was an experienced woodsman and made almost as good time going up as the guides could have made. It was not long before he was just beneath Louis, whom he instructed to climb a little higher.

Then he swung himself astride the limbs which Louis had occupied, and bending his head back, gazed at the spot to which the guide was pointing.

And well might the guide have shouted in his excitement, for attached jointly to trunk and limb, bound firmly into place with many yards of black tyre tape, was a heavy sporting-rifle—a Savage 30-30, as Blake discovered a little later.

Twisting round, he followed the line of the barrel, and, by screwing his head to one side and applying his eye to the stock, he found that it was directed full on the back of the canvas camp chair which had been occupied by Angus Carson when he was murdered.

But that was only the beginning of the startling discoveries Blake was to make during the next quarter of an hour.

After satisfying the eager curiosity of Stephen Hamilton and the doctor, he set to work to make a detailed examination of the rifle.

The first thing he noticed was that it was at full cock, and this, he discovered a moment later, was due to the fact that the rifle was of the automatic type, somewhat, after the pattern of the Winchester .401.

In the automatic action the recoil of the mechanism ejects the empty cartridge after the discharge, and on the recoil lifts another cartridge from the magazine, slipping it into the breech, and at the same time throws the hammer back to full cock, the action being practically similar to that of the automatic pistol.

The next thing that engaged Blake's attention was a most curious looking contrivance which had been attached to the stock of the rifle, and from which a thin piece of steel wire extended to the trigger, to which it was attached by a small loop that fitted tightly.

Blake was vastly intrigued to know the meaning of this, and he was just bending closer to pursue his examination more carefully when suddenly he saw the wire move backwards the veriest trifle, and before he had time to detect the cause, there came a low hiss as the hammer dropped.

Before Blake's astonished gaze the whole breech mechanism went through the full range of action, an empty cartridge was thrown out, a fresh one was engaged from the magazine and slipped into place, while the hammer was brought back to the full cock.

It was uncanny, to say the least, and yet before his very eyes the rifle had been discharged —or, rather, had discharged itself and the sound, he found on inquiry, had been scarcely audible to Stephen Hamilton and Dr. Taylor, who stood at the foot of the tree.

What was the explanation of this mystery? Blake knew positively that the rifle had not been discharged due to any action on his part. No part of his body had touched the weapon from the moment he had begun to investigate it.

He was too experienced in his profession to make a false move of that sort until the right moment came. And yet there could be not the slightest doubt that in some way the weapon had been discharged. It did not take him long to discover why the sound of the discharge had been practically negligible, for, as his eyes went along the barrel, he saw that something which he had previously noticed attached to the end was undoubtedly some form of silencer, although of a different type from the well-known silencer invented by Sir Hiram Maxim.

That explained how the sound had been suppressed, and if, as he now believed, this rifle was the one that had caused the death of Angus Carson, then in that silencer lay the explanation as to why no one had heard the sound of a shot fired when Carson was killed.

But while he quickly satisfied himself on that point, it was by no means as easy to explain the other puzzling problem.

That the unaided discharge had emanated from the curious-looking, box-like contrivance that was attached to the stock of the rifle, he did not doubt, for with his own eyes he had seen the wire tighten against the trigger, thus causing the mechanism to come into full action.

But what within that box had caused the movement of the wire?

Had it been caused by some vibration of the tree, due to his or the guide's movements? If not, then what could have caused it to act at that moment?

While he very cautiously lifted the barrel up until, in case there was another discharge, the bullet would take a course over the house, he requested Hamilton to go to the veranda and find where the bullet had struck.

The latter hurried across the open space, and from where he sat Blake could see him searching about the table.

Then he moved to the log wall of the house and took out his knife. Blake saw him pry something loose from one of the lower logs and come hurrying back to the clump of trees.

When he was once more beneath where Blake sat, he held up something between his fingers.

"I found it," he said. "It took a course just over the canvas back of the chair, went through the pine top of the table, and was stopped by one of the lower logs. It is the same sort of bullet that we found on poor old Carson."

"All right," Called Blake. "The rifle was at full cock, but I can't tell yet what discharged it.

"There is a curious box affair attached to the stock, which seems to have given the necessary motive power.

"I am going to detach the wire that runs from it to the trigger, and then I will lower the hammer. We will have no more accidental discharges."

Suiting the action to the word, he gently slipped the loop off the trigger and then lowered the hammer into place. That done, he motioned for Louis to climb down and hold the rifle while he unwound the tyre tape that held it in place.

The two below watched with interest while Blake worked, and when the rifle had been freed he tied one end of the long length of tape to the stock.

"Stand by!" he called. "I am going to lower it! Don't touch it any more than necessary!"

Foot by foot he lowered it between the branches until Hamilton could reach up and grasp it. Then Blake dropped the end of the tape which he held, and, signing to Louis to follow him, began to descend.

On reaching the ground, Blake did not at once pick up the rifle which Hamilton had laid on one side, but instructed Louis and Pierre to make a careful search of the ground at the foot of the tree.

It was soft all about with the soft mulch formed by the dropping fir needles over many years, but the two guides went at their work in a systematic manner that left not a single square inch unexamined.

Blake had picked up the empty cartridge that had been thrown out a few minutes before, and less than five minutes passed when Louis gave a grunt and stood up holding another empty cartridge, exactly similar, between the thumb and forefinger.

Blake took it and showed it to Stephen Hamilton and the physician.

"That was the cartridge which caused Angus Carson's death," he said briefly, as he dropped the two into his pocket. "Now let us go back to the house; we can examine this weapon more easily there."

They trooped back to the veranda, where Blake's first act was to remove the magazine and eject the cartridge which was in the breech. Then he laid the whole affair on the table and studied it closely.

The contrivance which was attached to the stock was of irregular shape, about six inches deep at the wider end and about four inches deep at the narrower end, which was also the end nearest the trigger-guard.

It was of mahogany, with none of its mechanism visible excepting a most curious-looking cylinder of metal which had been attached to one side.

It was on this that Blake was concentrating his attention, and so long did he study it that both Stephen Hamilton and the physician shifted impatiently.

But Blake was not to be hurried.

Neither of the others had ever seen him in action in this sort of a case, and they could not know that his mind was far away from where he stood at that moment.

For that curious-looking metal cylinder had suggested a line of thought to Blake that had sent his mind delving into a science of which he himself was no mean exponent.

The suggestion that had come to him was so startling as to be almost unbelievable. And yet, if what he was beginning to think was the force that had caused the mechanism of the rifle to act even as he gazed at it, he knew that not only was it entirely possible but that it also eliminated at once any possibility that any one of the French-Canadian guides could be guilty.

For if he should be able to show that his suspicions were correct, then the whole affair could only be the work of an individual of considerable scientific attainments.

But if he had been able to hold any doubt about Stephen Hamilton, which, of course, he hadn't, he would also have ruled out Hamilton, for he knew that the bluff operator was utterly incapable of the finesse required for carrying through such a fiendishly clever crime.

Abruptly he turned to speak to Hamilton, but even as he opened his lips he closed them again, for he had caught a glimpse of something white as it flashed from view through the open doorway that gave on to the living-room.

In two strides Blake was at the door, and was just in time to see Kamoto, the Jap, disappearing into the bed-room where his dead master lay. Blake called to him sharply.

The Jap came obediently, and Blake ordered him to follow him to the veranda.

"Kamoto has already seen what we have here," he said carelessly to Hamilton, "so he might as well remain."

"But I don't understand, Blake," exclaimed Hamilton. "What is it all about? What is the meaning of that affair on the stock of the rifle?"

"I will explain presently," answered Blake. Then he turned to the Japanese.

"Ever seen anything like that?" he asked, in the valet's own tongue, pointing to the box-like affair as he spoke.

The Jap gazed for a few moments at the object, then he turned his passive countenance towards Blake. His answer, startled the latter considerably.

"Yes, honourable sir."

Blake was so amazed that he hesitated for a moment before proceeding with his questions. Finally he said:

"You know what it is?"

"Yes, sir."

"Have you ever seen one in use?"

"No, honourable sir, but I have seen a working model of one."

"Have you ever seen this one before?" demanded Blake harshly.

Again came that baffling flicker in the Jap's eyes, but his denial came smoothly.

"No, honourable sir."

"You cannot guess how it came there?"

Once more the flicker, and once, more the denial.

"Tell me in your own tongue what it is," ordered Blake.

The man replied swiftly, describing in a few words exactly what the object was, and how it could be worked. And in each detail his explanation was in entire agreement with Blake's own opinion.

Blake was more convinced than ever that there was something decidedly queer about the Jap's association with the affair, and yet up to now there was not a single thing on which he could put his finger.

He knew how futile it would be to suggest having the man arrested on suspicion, for, in the absence of actual proof, no cross examination would entangle the controlled tongue of the Oriental.

And yet Blake was most anxious to get hold of some definite clue before the arrival of the sheriff, for he knew how that well-meaning but not over-intelligent officer would blunder if he had the slightest suspicion against anyone.

Precipitate action might upset the whole inquiry, and in order that he might be free to trace the subtle mind that had conceived this ghastly crime, Blake was almost ready that Stephen Hamilton should be arrested on suspicion so that the guilty person might be thrown off his guard, thus making him more likely to commit a blunder.

He did not pursue his questions then, but turning back to Hamilton said:

"I believe I know the nature of this contrivance which is attached to the stock. But before explaining just what connection it had with the murder of Angus Carson, I wanted to find out if Kamoto could tell me what it was."

"And could he?"

"He described it with a clearness that would have done credit to a specialist. And now, Hamilton, if you will instruct Kamoto to bring me a screwdriver, I shall demonstrate exactly how Angus Carson was murdered."

When the Jap had brought the required instrument, Blake bent over the stock of the rifle and began to unscrew the small corner screws that held one side of the mahogany box in place.

When he had lifted it clear, he pointed to the interior which, however, did not seem to enlighten either Stephen Hamilton or the doctor,

"What you see before you," went on Blake, in a conversational tone, "is nothing more or less than a small, but very effective, wireless receiving instrument.

"Now that the box is open, you can see here where the wave having been caught by the receiver which is attached to the outside of the box, is communicated to this interior mechanism, and how the subsequent action acts on this thin wire that passes through the box and was attached to the trigger of the rifle.

"It is altogether extremely simple, and I have not the slightest doubt that the murder of Angus Carson was very deliberately, and, I might say, very cleverly planned.

"Very considerable thought must have been applied to the working out of the details.

"For instance, let us trace back just what the murderer would have to consider.

"Firstly, we must presume that, having some strong motive for wishing to get rid of Angus Carson, he cast about for some means of accomplishing his object without directing suspicion towards himself.

"We must take it that he was no mean scientist, either amateurish or professionally— we don't know which. At any rate, he was well versed in wireless phenomena, and, in seeking a means to kill his intended victim, he pondered the possibilities of turning this knowledge to his purpose.

"Having hit upon his scheme, he would next take steps to test it out, and. since it was successful in its ultimate trial, we must suppose that his experiments were highly encouraging.

"Next for a venue. We must conclude that he had an intimate knowledge of Carson's daily habits, and he must have known for some time that Carson would be coming to this camp on Caribou Lake with you, Hamilton. That enables us to narrow things down a bit.

"Following that, we can picture our would-be murderer secretly surveying the ground here and then waiting until his victim should arrive. But that was by no means all he must learn.

"He would have to know to a fine point the daily habits of your camp and make a test of them over several days.

"Once he was able to count on his victim doing a certain thing at a certain time every day, then he would set his trap.

"What he ultimately chose was the time when you and Carson took your meals, and he must have known that Carson invariably sat in the same place.

"I don't know that that was so, but I am prepared to say that it is likely."

"By heavens, you are right!" exclaimed Hamilton, who, together with the doctor, had been hanging on Blake's cool statement of the matter. "He always sat in that canvas camp-chair at the end of the table."

Blake nodded.

"His murderer knew that and counted on it. Very well, let us proceed. The next step was to get the rifle fixed in place, and in this the very finest work was essential. The man who affixed that rifle to the limb of that tree and aimed it at the required spot was a master marksman. Another fact for us.

"Then, with all prepared, he had to have two factors in his favour before he could count with any degree of certainty on the success of his plan.

"The first was that he must know positively that his victim was seated in his usual place at the time the rifle was discharged, and, secondly, he must have a perfectly calm moment for the discharge of the rifle.

"Even a slight breeze would disturb the branch to which the rifle was attached, thus throwing the bullet wide of the mark.

"And bear in mind all the time that the murderer was operating from some distance. I am not prepared yet even to attempt to guess how far away the point of causation was, but it was either sufficiently within your camp circle to make the risk of discovery negligible, or else it was far enough away to ensure the same security.

"Nor have I named all the factors that might militate against the murderer's success.

"He had even to chance that a squirrel would not be running along the limb at that fatal moment, or that a bird did not disturb it. He took all those chances and he won out.

"So the problem before us is, firstly, to bring within the circle of suspicion all those persons who might be capable of evolving and carrying out such a subtle scheme.

"Secondly, we must discover the exact point of causation. When we have accomplished those two things, we shall find ourselves close on the track of the man who murdered Angus Carson, or I shall be forced to own myself very badly astray in my deductions.

"'That, gentlemen, is all I have to say at present. I would suggest, Hamilton, that you lock this rifle and the attachment carefully away until the arrival of the sheriff.

"And now, if you will excuse me, I am going for a walk in the woods. I want to give this matter further thought."

With that, Blake swung off the veranda and made for the belt of timber, leaving Stephen Hamilton and the doctor in a state of complete bewilderment from trying to grasp the rapid fire of his deductions.

THE FIFTH CHAPTER.   The Night Hunters—The Shot in the
Dark —Tinker is Angry—A Midnight Visitor.

TINKER and the young French Canadian made the journey to Black Water practically without incident.

The only thing that Tinker took note of was just as they were paddling out of Caribou into the strip of water that led to Black Water.

Off to the left, about half a mile away, he caught sight of a canoe containing one man. It was proceeding along close to the shore at a leisurely pace, and in reply to his question, young St. Pierre said:

"Zat ver' mooch lak bateau zat I sink belong' M'sieu Sweeney. Me, I sink M'sieu Sweeney mos' lakly in ze woods an' zat his guide follow in ze bateau."

If what the young fellow said was correct, then it seemed to Tinker that Ralph Sweeney and his guide had not wasted much time in picking up their guns and starting out, for it was not long since they had left the other camp.

But he knew it was not likely young St. Pierre would be mistaken.

While he himself could barely make out the fact that the canoe contained but a single occupant, the young woodsman could tell practically every detail about the craft, owing to the training he had had from babyhood.

They soon lost sight of it as they slipped along the connecting strip of water towards Black Water, and as they sent their own craft dancing along towards the opposite shore, where the St. Pierre cabin stood, Tinker forgot all about it.

There was a short delay at the St. Pierre's while the buckboard was hitched up, but it was not long before they were bumping along over the cordouroy road on the way to Plaster Rock.

On their arrival at the settlement, Tinker went first to the railroad station, where he despatched his telegram to Lindsay, Blake's Montreal agent.

That done, he made inquiries about the evening train due from Aroostook Junction.

The operator at the station informed him that it would be late, as the up line was blocked by a freight train, that had run off the metals.

When he had gone to the general store, which was also the post-office, to inquire for mail for Stephen Hamilton, he decided that he would try and get back to the camp that night and leave word for the sheriff to follow on in the morning.

There was still a good hour of daylight yet remaining, so he figured they ought to be able to cover the worst part of the road before it was dark.

And he knew it would not be very difficult to make the canoe part of the journey by the light of the stars, as Napoleon St. Pierre and his sons knew every foot of the way.

Therefore, he climbed back into the buckboard and they started off.

He had not figured wrong, for they made the ten miles or so in excellent time, due principally to the fact that the two wiry little horses were anxious to get home to their own stable.

The St. Pierre family were just sitting down to the evening meal of pork and beans, and, as Tinker knew none of them would come with him until after supper, he sat down with them and put away his share of the plain but well-cooked fare without the slightest difficulty.

It was just a little after nine o'clock when they got started. The same young fellow who had brought Tinker from the camp volunteered to accompany him back, so, after arranging with Napoleon St. Pierre to provide a canoe for the next day, they sent the canoe towards the distant shore at a good steady clip.

Almost before it seemed possible, the young fellow gave the sign to proceed more slowly, as they were about to enter the strip of water that led to Caribou.

Tinker lifted his paddle out of the water and held it across his knees while the young guide took them round the bend and into the passage with a single paddle.

They were about half-way along, and Tinker was just about to dip his paddle back into the water, when the young guide gave vent to a low exclamation, which caused Tinker to sit with his paddle poised just above the surface of the water.

His companion, who sat behind him, also stopped paddling, and as they swept on silently, Tinker suddenly saw what had caused the other to exclaim.

Off to the right, and apparently among the trees which grew close to the edge of the water, he caught sight of a light.

It appeared to be moving slowly, just above the surface of the water, close to the shore, and when his companion uttered another low-voiced exclamation, Tinker grasped what it meant.

Someone was out night-hunting.

Tinker knew it could be no one from Stephen Hamilton's camp. Even without the tragedy there, he knew that neither Stephen Hamilton nor any of his men would go night-hunting.

He was just asking himself who it could be, when suddenly there was a flash, and almost at the same instant his paddle was jerked out of his hand as the crack of a rifle sounded.

Tinker made an involuntary grab for the paddle, forgetting how ticklish a craft the canoe is, with the result that, although young St. Pierre cried out a warning, the canoe went over, precipitating Tinker and his companion into the water.

And well it was that the accident had happened just when it did, for, even as they went over, another crack sounded and a bullet ripped into the water just over their heads.

Tinker came to the surface, spluttering and incensed at the person or persons who apparently knew so little of woodcraft that they would shoot indiscriminately at night.

Nor did he hesitate to express his opinion while the young guide swam round, looking for the paddles.

"Hi, you darned idiot!" called Tinker. "What the dickens do you think you are trying to do? Are you trying to commit murder?"

There was a momentary silence, then came a voice that Tinker at once recognised as that of Ralph Sweeney.

"Good heavens!" he exclaimed. "We thought it was a moose. Are you all right? Hang on, and we will paddle out to you."

"Zere is no need, m'sieu," called St. Pierre. "We can mak' ze swim."

Tinker turned, and saw that the canoe was close to him. He had been treading water, but now he grabbed hold of the craft, and together they pushed it towards the shore.

As they waded out they saw the light approaching them, and a few moments later Ralph Sweeney and his guide were beside them.

"I am most awfully sorry," said Sweeney suavely. "I do hope you are not injured. Oh, it is you, my lad. I thought there was something familiar about your voice. I trust you will understand that I greatly regret the accident. We were night-hunting, and certainly took your canoe for a moose."

Tinker said nothing until he had helped his companion to empty the water out of the canoe and launch it. Then he turned to Sweeney.

"You are much older than I am, Mr. Sweeney, and therefore I can't speak as freely as I might to someone nearer my own age. But I will say this much.

"Any full grown man who prowls round the woods at night and shoots at a canoe, thinking it is a moose, ought to have a nurse with him. As for your guide, there is no excuse whatsoever for him, and I shall jolly well see that he loses his licence over this!"

"Now, now, now, my boy," said Sweeney, with a jovial laugh, "don't take it so seriously. It was all my fault, and I am very sorry for it. It was an unfortunate occurrence that might happen to anyone."

"You are entitled to your opinion, Mr. Sweeney, and, incidentally, I shall be glad if you will not call me 'my lad,' or 'my boy.' Only my friends have that privilege.

"You say it was a mistake, and I repeat, my opinion. And before I go I will say this— if there are any more 'mistakes' like that, someone is going to get drilled good and plenty!"

With that Tinker swung his revolver round from where it hung in the hollow of his left shoulder.

"That goes for your guide, too," he said.

He said no more, but again took his place in the canoe, and held his paddle poised until young St. Pierre had also stepped in.

Then they sent the craft shooting away across the starlit waters, followed by the low laugh of Ralph Sweeney. Not until they were fully half-way back to the camp did Tinker speak. Then he said:

"What do you think of that affair back there, St. Pierre?"

"Me, m'sieu, I sink eet ees ver' strange that wan man should shoot at ze canoe for ze moose.

"You, m'sieu, you mak' true talk; but tak' ze teep from me, m'sieu, an 'look out for zat guide! 'E ees wan bad fellow!"

"I'll watch out for him all right," answered Tinker grimly.

"Eet ees strange, too, m'sieu, zat zay shoot w'en zay mos' 'ave 'ear ze chanson."

"Jiminy, you are right!" exclaimed Tinker suddenly. "You were singing the whole way across the lake, and didn't stop until just before we paddled into the connecting strip of water. You have said something there, St. Pierre. On this still night air they must have heard you plainly."

"Me, zat ees w'at I sink also, m'sieu. Zen, too, m'sieu, we mak' no soun'. Eet ees ver' plain from w'ere zay stan' zat eet ees wan canoe. Ze moose, 'e mak' ver' begg noise in ze water, an' canoe she no look lak' moose swim'. W'at you sink, m'sieu?"

"I think you are dead right," answered Tinker. "Of course, they could see the canoe as a shadow against the water from where they stood. And they couldn't possibly mistake it for moose. I believe there is something wrong there."

"Eet look lak zat, m'sieu, but don't forget zat zer are many beeg fools in ze woods. Ver' offen zay shoot ze man for ze deer."

"Yes, that is true," admitted Tinker. "All the same, I don't like it; but I can't imagine why the dickens they would want to shoot at us."

"Zat guide ees wan bad man! 'Im e shoot ver' queek eef he haf troubl' wis ozer man."

There may have been a good deal suspicious about the occurrence, but Tinker realised that whatever the truth might be he would never be able to prove it.

All the same, it was a little queer that such a thing should happen just after he had sent a confidential telegram of inquiry to Montreal regarding one of the actors in the affair. After deciding that he would get Blake's opinion on it, he dismissed it from his mind.

Although they were both soaked to the skin when the canoe had capsized, the steady action of paddling had almost dried there clothes, and as they drew near the camp Tinker gave the word to go slow.

"They will probably all be in bed," he said, in a low tone. "No need to wake them. I can slip across and into the house without disturbing them. What will you do, St. Pierre? Will you stay here to-night, or are you going back to Black Water."

"Me I weel go back, m'sieu. I s'all paddle ver' slow, an', besides, I may see ze two mens zat mak' ze shoot."

"Good idea, St. Pierre! If you hear or see anything, you might let me know."

"I tell you ver' queek, m'sieu."

The canoe grounded almost noiselessly a few moments later, and Tinker stepped out. He said good-night, and waited until Pierre had swung the craft free, and stared back; then he turned and stole softly across the sand that lay between him and the house.

As he thought, the place was in darkness except for a faint light that shone out from a window on the south side of the building.

But this he knew was in the room where the body of Angus Carson lay, and he did not think anyone would be sitting up there.

He reached the veranda, and tiptoed softly along to the corner near which the dining-table stood.

Ordinarily, he knew that the main door would have been wide open to the night, since the tragedy Stephen Hamilton had secured it, as Tinker knew from a remark Hamilton had made.

Reaching the corner, he passed round the table, then continued along the veranda on the north side, intending to reach his room by way of the window. But he had taken less than half a dozen steps when he drew up sharply, and stood peering off towards the grove of trees which stood not far away.

Then he dropped softly to the ground, and began working his way across towards the clump, for he was now certain that he had caught a momentary glimpse of a light somewhere among the trees.

Who could be making a surreptitious visit there at that hour of the night, he asked himself.

As Blake and Tinker crawled nearer they saw the outline of a human figure down on its knees intently studying something before it. No stranger sight had ever been seen in the big woods than that at which they were now gazing. What did it all mean? (*Chapter 6.*)

THE SIXTH CHAPTER. An Unprovoked Attack—A Misunderstanding—The Shrine in the Forest—The Lacquered Box.

WHEN he had covered a few yards, Tinker dropped flat to the ground, and went squirming along, Red Indian fashion. He had got another glimpse of the light, and, as far as he could make out, it was stationary.

Naturally, he knew nothing of the surprising discoveries which had been made by Blake after his departure for Plaster Rock.

If he had, he would have seen that the light in the grove was just about at the spot above which Blake had come upon the murder contraption.

Even so, Tinker knew that, in some way, Blake had felt that there was some connection between the grove and the murder, for there had been not the slightest doubt, even after a preliminary examination, that the bullet had come from that direction.

Therefore he was more than a little intrigued to know who could have business there at that hour of the night—business which it seemed, must be attended to while the household slept.

When he reached the edge of the clump he paused for a few moments while he made an exact location of the light.

He could not make out any signs of a human being near it, nor was the light bright enough to throw much illumination beyond its immediate surroundings.

Yet the very fact that the light was there pointed to some human agency as being the cause and, when one considered the mystery that surrounded the camp, it behoved him to find out just what that human agency was. At least, so Tinker figured.

He started on again, but now his progress was necessarily much slower, for he knew that whoever was in the grove would be on guard against interruption, and if, by chance, that same person had any connection with the murder of Angus Carson then Tinker realised only too well that for the second time that night his life might be in jeopardy.

As far as he could judge, his objective was some twenty-five or thirty feet on from the edge of the trees.

He had covered about a quarter of this distance, and had sunk close to the ground, when suddenly there was a faint stirring of the bushes on his right.

He started to cock his head to find out what could have caused the sound, when the next moment something jammed into the small of his back, while a pair of hands gripped his throat, completely shutting off any effort he might make to cry out.

"One move out of you, and I will choke you senseless." hissed a voice in his ear. "Move aside into the bushes here."

As Tinker heard the words he followed the urging of the other's hands and rolled over slowly, while his captor dragged him aside from the path.

Inch by inch he was forced along until he was a full yard or so from the path, then his assailant bent over him, and Tinker could feel the eyes boring through the darkness trying to discern his features.

He lifted one of his hands and tapped his captor on the arm. As if understanding the meaning of the action, the other relaxed his throttling grip somewhat, and, as the blessed air filled his lungs once more, Tinker gasped in a whisper:

"Guv'nor, it's me, Tinker! Nearly choked me senseless!"

Even before he finished the sentence, the hands at his throat were removed and he felt Blake drop down beside him. Then he heard Blake speaking close beside his ear.

"You Tinker! What on earth are you doing here? I had no idea you were returning to-night!"

"I found I could make it, so come on," panted Tinker. "I saw the light in the grove here, so thought I would investigate. What is it?"

"I think I know but am not sure yet," breathed Blake. "I was just investigating when I heard you behind me. I am going on now to find out what it means.

"Follow me if you can, but mind, no noise."

Blake started to crawl away, and, rolling over, Tinker followed him. The light was still to be seen at the same spot, and as they drew nearer they could see that a human figure was undoubtedly close to it. But is was the position of the figure that puzzled them.

It was neither standing nor lying nor moving about, but seemed to be on its knees studying something. Blake risked discovery by crawling forward until he was within ten feet of the light; then suddenly he paused, and laid a cautioning hand on Tinker's arm.

Tinker worked his way up beside Blake, and then saw what had brought his master to a stop. And well it might, for no stranger sight had ever been seen in the big woods than that at which they were now gazing. At the foot of the tree where Blake had found the murder-trap, had been set up his astonished eyes now made out was a small statue of the Buddha.

It seemed to be resting in some sort of lacquer chest, while on either side of it burned two quivers of joss-sticks. And to complete the amazing scene, they saw Kimoto the Japanese valet, kneeling before it in deep contemplation, while off to one side stood the small lantern which gave forth the light that had attracted their attention. There was something very sinister in that picture of Eastern worship in the big, clean woods. Both Blake and Tinker knew instinctively that this midnight contemplation of a pagan god had some very real connection with the murder of Angus Carson.

To Blake's mind it definitely linked up the valet with the death of his master. But how? And what was the real meaning of that scene before them? What part had the valet played in the crime? And what did this new phase portend?

Those were the questions Sexton Blake was asking himself as he signed to Tinker to make back for the house.

They crept away, leaving the Oriental to his contemplation. They reached Blake's rooms without rousing any of the sleeping household. But they did not go to bed. Instead, they sat in the darkness waiting and watching, until just as the first faint streak of dawn appeared in the East, they saw a figure slink out of the grove and steal across to the sleeping-shack at the back of the house.

It was the valet, and beneath his arm he carried a lacquered box.

The sheriff straightened himself and thrust what seemed to be a mahogany box towards the startled Stephen Hamilton and Dr. Taylor. "Har!" he leered. "Perhaps yer smart detective friend from Lunnon can tell us what this is!" (*Chapter* 7.)

THE SEVENTH CHAPTER.   The Sheriff Arrives —And Proves Unpleasant —The Sheriff's Find —Arrested —Blake Speaks Out.

DESPITE the fact that it was dawn before they finally turned in, both Blake and Tinker were up and dressed by seven o'clock.

They found Stephen Hamilton standing on the veranda with a pair of binoculars focused on the lake, and, following his gaze, they could just make out a small dark patch to the south that seemed to be increasing rapidly in size.

When Hamilton had greeted them he handed the glasses to Blake, who then was able to make out that the dark speck was a canoe in which were three persons, two of whom were paddling at high speed.

"That will be Sheriff Maxwell," remarked Hamilton, when Blake had lowered the glasses "The other two are probably two of Napoleon St. Pierre's boys."

Blake nodded.

"Has Dr. Taylor appeared yet?" he asked.

"Yes; he is in Carson's room seeing that everything is all right. As soon as the sheriff has made his examination, we shall have to make immediate arrangements about the burial."

"Have you decided where—"

"Yes—Plaster Rock. I don't think it would serve any good purpose to send the body to Montreal. I can get the Methodist parson up from Perth to carry out the service.

"My heavens! I shall be glad when this is all over Blake. Your discovery yesterday afternoon has unnerved me. Have you any idea of a clue yet? You know the sheriff may not be so ready to believe in my innocence as others.

"The fact remains that all you have discovered goes to prove more strongly than ever that it was foul murder, and you can't get away from the ominous truth that I was the only person near Carson when the shot was fired."

"I have nothing definite to say yet," responded Blake. "Cheer up, Hamilton, I know that you didn't do it, and, even if we can't persuade the sheriff to look at things in the same light, you will never come for trial on the charge of murdering Angus Carson. I give you my word on that score.

"I have more than one idea, but it is too early yet for me to commit myself. Then don't forget that we have absolute proof that the rifle was unquestionably discharged by means of a wireless wave."

"Yes, but the sheriff may consider that I was the one who was responsible for that."

"How can he when you don't possess a wireless set? Why, you haven't even an ordinary listening-in set, have, you?"

"No; I have thought of getting one for the camp here, in order to try and pick up some of the broadcasting from the big stations, but I found that a very powerful one would be necessary owing to the great distance of the camp from the nearest broadcasting station, so I gave up the idea."

Sexton Blake gazed thoughtfully in the direction of the approaching canoe.

"It was undoubtedly one of the most subtle crimes it has ever been my lot to come across," he said slowly. "Why, it might be regarded in half a dozen different ways.

"What we must first discover is the exact wave-length to which the receiving-set on the rifle was tuned. Owing to the fact that it was necessarily of a small size, I do not believe that the point from which the operating wave emanated was very far distant, speaking of distance from a wireless point of view.

"Then again, it is by no means beyond the range of possibility that the rifle might have been discharged by a chance wave from one of the big stations, say, for instance, the one at Glace Bay, in Nova Scotia.

"That would be the nearest wireless station to your camp. But, of course, the chances against that would be enormous, as the first requirement would be that the instrument attached to the rifle was tuned to the same wave-length—a thing that would be very unlikely.

"No, Hamilton, the more I consider the whole devilish scheme the more convinced am I that the wave which operated the mechanism was sent with full murderous intent at a moment when the murderer knew for a positive fact that Angus Carson was sitting in the chair on which the rifle had been trained.

"And in order that it might be discharged at that psychological moment and no other the murderer would be careful to have the receiving set tuned to a length which would put it outside the risk of being discharged by a chance wave from one of the big stations.

"That is the most difficult problem we have before us. And while it is not to be easy to locate that sending-station, we must do it somehow.

"And now I see that Sheriff Maxwell is landing. We shall soon know what he thinks of the affair."

Dr. Taylor joined them just then, and all eyes were turned on the short, rugged-looking man who was striding towards them.

He was dressed as any lumberjack might have dressed, with the exception that his broad-brimmed Stetson was of better quality than the ordinary woodsman could afford.

It was plain that he was a victim to the tobacco-chewing habit, for as he came along he expectorated with rather disgusting frequency.

He did not lift his eyes towards the group on the veranda until he had mounted it. Then, as he recognised Dr. Taylor, he nodded, after which he turned to Stephen Hamilton.

Hamilton had never met the sheriff, but the other had seen Hamilton more than once.

"Well, Mr. Hamilton," be said brusquely, in a strong nasal twang, "I got your telegram, and I heerd in Plaster Rock some rumours of what has happened here. Where is the corpse?"

"I will take you in presently, sheriff," responded Hamilton a little curtly, for the other's disregard of even the most primitive courtesies had angered him.

"First let me introduce you to my guest, Mr. Blake of London, and to his assistant. You already know Dr. Taylor."

"Pleased tu meet yu!" snapped the sheriff, as he nodded to Blake. Then: "What do yu need an assistant for, hell? Is this young heifer your valet?"

"You have misunderstood me, sheriff," answered Stephen Hamilton stiffly. "Mr. Blake, I should have explained, is Mr. Sexton Blake, a very famous London criminologist, and this young man is his assistant."

The sheriff screwed up his face and gave vent to a loud guffaw.

"Har, har!" he cackled. "I've heerd of you, Mr. Detective. You are the feller that uses them gol-danged, new-fangled notions— jest play-actin', let me tell yu!

"The good old methods are the best—jest let yer Uncle Dudley tell yu. Now, then, Mr. Hamilton, I ain't gut no time tu waste. Let's have a look at the corpse. 'N I guess Mr. London Creemeenoleegeest, yu and yer assistant kin stay out hyar.

"This is a case fer the law—not fer any danged foolishness!"

Stephen Hamilton's face flamed, but Blake shot him a look that caused him to suppress the remarks he was about to make. Dr. Taylor also flushed with shame at the sheriff's rudeness to a man whom he looked up to with the deepest respect.

But he knew no sarcasm could ever penetrate the thick hide of Sheriff Maxwell, so he held his peace.

As a matter of fact, both Blake and Tinker were more amused than anything else at the other's rudeness and his provincial cocksureness. At the same time, his attitude made Blake a little uneasy on Hamilton's account.

He and Tinker remained on the veranda while the sheriff stumped away on the heels of Hamilton and the doctor.

Blake had already given Tinker a brief account of his discoveries the previous afternoon, but while they waited he described in detail just what he had found and the theory he had evolved from it.

When he had finished, Tinker, for the first time, told Blake what had happened the night before, when he and young St. Pierre were on their way from Black Water to Caribou.

Blake questioned the lad closely on every point; then he grew very thoughtful. His musings were interrupted by the loud voice of the sheriff as he returned from his examination of the body.

"Now, then, Mr. Hamilton," he was saying, "I'll just hear your version of what happened. I'll tell yu, tu begin with, that I agree with yu on one point.

"The murdered man was shot in the back all right, and, believe me, we will soon have the murderer. Now, jest let's hev the yarn."

Stephen Hamilton related in detail the same story he had already told Blake. He described how he and Angus Carson had sat down to lunch at the usual time, and how, at the completion of the meal, he had got up to go into the living-room for a box of cigars.

Then he described how, on his return, he had made the ghastly discovery that during the few moments he had been inside his friend had been shot.

The sheriff expectorated freely during the recital, but he did not interrupt. But when Hamilton had finished, he said:

"I understand yu tu say thet yu didn't hyar any sound of a shot."

"That is so."

"Well, thet's suttunly danged queer, fer, as an old gun-hand, I kin tell yu, Mr. Hamilton, thet the shot was fired from purty close."

"I thoroughly agree with that," answered Hamilton curtly. "If you will wait until you hear all, you will perhaps understand why no one heard the shot.

"I have already told you that Mr. Sexton Blake, who is an old friend of mine, was on his way to the camp to pay me a visit.

"Soon after the tragedy, I went into Plaster Rock and on to Aroostook Junction, where I met Mr. Blake and his assistant. I telegraphed for you at the same time.

"I also saw Dr. Taylor on the train, and asked him to come out to the camp. When we arrived here—that is, after the doctor had made his examination—I requested Mr. Blake, as a friend of mine, to make an investigation while we awaited your arrival."

"Har, yu did, did yu? Yu had no business tu do that. There hain't nuthin' about this consarns this here feller from London.

"I'm the sheriff of this county, by heck, and I'll hev yu tu understand that! But go on! In jest what way hev things ben muddled?"

"You may be sheriff of this county, but your position does not give you any authority to come here and insult my guests, even though you may be here in an official capacity!" snapped Hamilton angrily. "I will thank you to put more restraint on your tongue!"

"Yu will, will yu? Best look out, Mr. Hamilton, that I don't put this restraint on yu!

"Yu jest remember what I hev said, and let me hyar the rest danged quick! Then I'll let you know what I think."

Hamilton shrugged. Then he went on wearily with his tale. He spoke of how Blake had drawn certain deductions from the course the bullet had taken, and how the result of those deductions had been the discovery of the rifle in the fir-tree.

At that point the sheriff insisted on seeing the rifle, and there was a halt in the proceedings while Hamilton went to fetch it.

There was no question that he knew guns well enough, for he made his examination in a highly professional manner, and revealed an intelligent knowledge of the type of silencer used.

"That is why no sound of a shot was heard," said Hamilton. "While Mr. Blake was examining it up in the tree, it was accidentally discharged again, and, on locating where the bullet struck, we proved that Mr. Blake's theory was correct, for the course was very similar to that taken by the one that had killed Mr. Carson."

"Yep I get yu there. But what I want tu know is why yu took this rifle down from the tree. Yu hed no business touchin' it before I got here."

"You can hold me responsible for that," put in Blake, speaking for the first time. "I have handled a good many cases touching on all forms of crime, and in every country in the world, and I am perfectly capable of vowing when evidence should not be disturbed, Mr. Sheriff.

"I am quite sure that you could have found nothing more had the rifle been left in the tree than we are able to place at your disposal."

"Yu think so, do yu? Let's jest see, then, how much yu kin tell me. What is this hyar contraption on the stock?"

"Isn't it perfectly obvious?" asked Blake coolly. "Have you ever seen a wireless receiving set, sheriff?"

"Perhaps I hev, and perhaps I hevn't. But yu seem tu want tu air yer knowledge, so jest spill the works, Mr. Detective!"

"Where is ignorance is bliss—" murmured Blake in a voice that only Tinker caught. Then aloud he said:

"I don't mind satisfying your curiosity, sheriff I shall be glad to give any information that will help in running down the man who killed Mr. Carson.

"That contraption, as you term it, is a small but very effective wireless receiving set.

"I have not had an opportunity yet to discover what wave length it is tuned to receive on, but, if you will follow me, I shall explain how, by being agitated to a wave sent from some unknown sending station, this delicate mechanism here was made to operate this wire which ran from the instrument along under the stock and so to the trigger.

"With the rifle affixed in place and set at full cock, the action of the wire drew the trigger back, and, of course, the rifle was at once discharged. Is that plain?"

"I get yu all right. What yu say may or may not be true. I'll be able tu decide that later. But, jest supposin' it is true, then yu gut tu show me more then thet.

"Mr. Hamilton says he was here alone with the man who was killed. He also says that they couldn't find any traces of anyone hangin' about the place. The only thing they saw was a canoe away out on the lake."

"That is so."

"Then I guess yu bring it right down tu brass tacks, Mr. Detective! As fur as I kin see, even if this hyar rifle was fired as yu say, it could only hev ben fired by someone right hyar in this camp."

"But that is impossible, Mr. Hamilton has already told you that he was living-room when the shot was fired.

"And the four men in his employ were all in the cookhouse at their midday meal. Besides, you lose sight of the fact that in order to operate the mechanism a sending set was essential."

"No, I hain't lost sight of thet. How do yu know there hain't no sich set hyar? Hev yu looked?"

"No. But it is not reasonable to suppose that any of the four men in Mr. Hamilton's employ would have a set, and Mr. Hamilton certainly hasn't one."

"Perhaps I'll agree with thet when I hev had a look myself. The first thing we will do is tu hev the four men lined up. We might jest call them hyar, Mr. Hamilton."

Stephen Hamilton walked to the end of the veranda and gave a call. A few moments later Louis put in an appearance and Hamilton instructed him to call the others. When they were lined up, the sheriff stood before them, glowering fiercely.

"Now yu listen tu me," he snarled. "Thar's ben murder dun hyar, and I'm a-goin' tu find out who did it. So let me warn yu to talk with a straight tongue.

"I'll take yu three Canucks first. What du yu know about it? Was yu all havin yer dinner, as yer boss says?"

Louis acted as spokesman for the three French Canadians. He gave his evidence quickly, and although the sheriff browbeat him time and again, the guide was unshaken in his story.

Then the sheriff turned his attention to the Jap valet. Blake knew about how much he would be able to get out of Komato.

"Yu was 'valley' tu the dead man, wasn't yu, Li Hung Chang?" he asked.

"Yes, honourable sir."

"Har! Now, then, Li Hung Chang—"

"Pardon me, honourable sir, I am Japanese man, not Chinese man."

"Har! It's all the same tu me. Yu jest answer my questions,

Chinkie, Do yu know anything about this murder?"

"No. honourable sir."

"Do yu suspect anyone?"

"No, honourable sir."

"Do yu know what this is." And the sheriff pointed to the wireless attachment.

"I understand what it is, honourable sir."

"Har! Yu do, do yu! Wal, then, yu know how yer master was killed?"

"Not before the honourable gentleman" —and he indicated Blake— "explained yesterday."

"Yu never saw this before, then?"

"No, honourable sir."

"Wal, yu kin all jest stay right hyar until I hev a look round. Doc, I want yu tu come with me. And yu better come, too, Mr. Hamilton."

The three of them entered the house, and passing through the bunk shack adjoining the cookhouse, began a search of the belongings of the four employees.

It took a very brief time to go through the dunnage of the three French Canadians, for their belongings were very scanty, and contained not the slightest thing to arouse suspicion.

Then the sheriff proceeded to examine Kamoto's box. Almost the first thing the sheriff came upon was a big, lacquered cabinet, and when he had lifted it out he instructed Hamilton to call the Jap.

When Kamoto had put in an appearance he showed no reluctance to open the box, revealing as he did so a yellow statue of the Buddha, with some strips of coloured paper and a bunch of joss sticks beneath it.

In answer to the sheriff's questioning, he explained that all devout Buddhists carried a replica of the Buddha with them.

And while he snorted at what he termed the "tarnal heathens," the sheriff could make nothing of the discovery which even his limited intelligence told him was probably quite an ordinary thing—as indeed it was.

He did not know under what circumstances that idol had previously been taken out of the lacquered casket.

That practically exhausted the possibilities of the bunk shack, so the sheriff next turned his attention to the house proper.

He had already made a brief examination of the dead man's

luggage, and now he informed Stephen Hamilton that he wished to go through his boxes. Hamilton snorted, but made no serious objection.

He led the way into his room, and, taking out his keys, unlocked his boxes. He and Dr. Taylor stood aside while the sheriff plunged his hands into the nearest box and recklessly tossed the contents out on to the floor.

He drew a blank, however, and was equally unsuccessful with the second box. But he did not give up yet. He prided himself on being an efficient officer, did Sheriff Maxwell, so he tackled the third box with energy.

Out came Hamilton's shirts and underwear and clothes until the sheriff had almost reached the bottom.

There he paused for a moment, and appeared to be tugging at something. Then he straightened up, and as he turned round Stephen Hamilton and Dr. Taylor saw that he held in his arms what seemed to be a mahogany box of sorts, while around it was a tangle of wires and brass connections.

Sheriff Maxwell gazed at Stephen Hamilton with a sardonic eye.

"I don't know much about this new-fangled wireless game, Mr. Hamilton," he said, with a leer, "but perhaps yer smart friend from London kin enlighten me."

As he finished speaking he walked across and laid the box on the bed. Then he stepped to the door.

"Mr. Detective," he called, "yu might jest come here, will yu?"

A moment later Blake swung through the door leading to the veranda, and crossed the living-room to where the sheriff stood.

"What is it?" he asked curtly.

"I think yu said, Mr. Detective, thet Mr. Hamilton had no wireless contraption, didn't yu?"

"Yes. Why?"

"Will yu look at this and tell me what yu call it?"

As he finished speaking, the sheriff stood aside, and pointed to the bed. Blake gave a sharp glance towards Stephen Hamilton as he entered the room.

His host was standing like one stunned, and for the moment Blake could not understand what had happened. Then suddenly his eyes fell on the bed.

Swiftly he appraised the mahogany box and the tangle of wires and brass connections which were attached to it. Then he turned and faced the sheriff.

"You ask me what I call this," he said curtly. "I should say that it is part of a wireless set. Where did you find it?"

"Har! Not so fast, Mr. Detective. Will yu jest look a little more closely, and tell me if it would be possible to send with that machine as well as receive by it?"

Blake bent over the box, and made a brief examination of the construction. Then he looked up.

"As it is now it would not be possible to send by it," he said. "But with certain attachments which appear to be missing, and given the proper 'set-up,' it would be possible, although not for a very great distance."

"Har! Now I'll answer yer question, Mr. Detective. Yer asked me where I found it!

"Har! Jest rest yer peepers on thet there trunk, Mr. Detective. Thet's where I found it, and thet trunk belongs to yer friend, Mr. Hamilton!

"Yer thought yer friend didn't have any wireless sending set, hell? Then what du yu make of this? Har!"

Blake turned a bewildered gaze upon Stephen Hamilton.

"For Heaven's sake, what does he mean, Hamilton?" he asked sharply.

Hamilton made a gesture of helplessness.

"I know no more about that set than you, Blake!" he exclaimed. "I spoke the truth when I said I didn't possess one. It must have been planted on me!"

"Har! Thet'll be jest about enough out of yu!" snapped the sheriff.

Suddenly he strode forward, and, before any of the others could grasp his intention, he had snapped a pair of handcuffs on Stephen Hamilton's wrists.

"Jest remember the usual warnin', Mr. Hamilton!" he said harshly. "Ye're under arrest on suspicion of hevin' caused the wilful murder of one Angus Carson, an anythin' yer may say will be took down and used as evidence against yer.

"Yer worked yer game party slick, but yer didn't count on Steve Maxwell, by heck!"

"But this is utterly preposterous!" exclaimed Blake angrily. "Mr. Hamilton is no more capable of committing such a cold-blooded murder than you, sheriff!"

"Har! Yu will git a chance tu say yer say at the inquest, Mr. Detective! In the meantime, yu kin go ahead with yer playactin' methods, and get proof tu clear yer friend.

"But if yu ask me, yer friend is due fer a nice long spell, if he don't git a few feet of hemp round his neck!"

"Look here, Maxwell," broke in Dr. Taylor, "you are making a terrible mistake! Mr. Hamilton could never have committed this crime. You will be well advised to withdraw your charges while there is time.

"You can have no idea of Mr. Sexton Blake's standing in the world to speak to him in such fashion."

The sheriff worked off a chunk of tobacco, and worked it into his cheek.

"Say, doc," he said at last, "yu seem tu be fergittin' thet yu hold the position of coroner of this hyer county. It will be yer duty tu preside at the inquest, and, believe me, yu ain't agoin' tu do thet if yu feel beforehand thet the prisoner ain't guilty.

"Yu tek my advice, and keep yer trap closed."

"I will express myself as I choose until I am restrained by the opening of the inquest!" cried the doctor hotly. "I tell you that you are making an asinine mistake!

"You will only succeed in making yourself the laughing-stock of the whole province. You seem to forget what happened some three years ago when you were so cocksure that you had run a certain gang of smugglers to earth.

"You would do well to take heed from that mistake."

The sheriff turned a dull red, and glared angrily at the doctor. He did not like being reminded of that incident in which he had made a great mistake, and had been chaffed over it along the whole of the St. John river valley.

"Thet's jest enough out of yu!" he snarled. "This hyar man is agoin' tu gaol. It's a clear open and shut case, as yu will find out before I finish.

"And now, as sheriff of the county, I call on yu to assist me tu get the prisoner intu the canoe.

"You kin bring along thet contraption. It will be the chief evidence against him."

With that he gave a tug at Stephen Hamilton's wrist, and marched him out of the room. Blake followed to the veranda, and called to Hamilton:

"Don't worry, old man! I'll be at the inquest, and we will show up this crazy idiot for what he is!"

The sheriff paused.

"Yu think so, do yu, Mr. Smarty? Jest try it. And let me tell yu something else. Close yer trap on them sort of names."

"Why, you ivory-headed dumb-bell, if I told you in real English what I thought of you, you would choke on that quid of tobacco you have in your cheek!

"Before I finish with you, I shall do just what I said and more. And after that, if you have any more fight left in you, I shall be right on hand!"

The sheriff almost had an apoplectic fit as Blake jeered at him, but he swallowed his reply and marched his prisoner down to the canoe.

Tinker was highly delighted at Blake's remarks, for Blake very rarely allowed himself to give vent to his anger in such fashion.

But it was a case where finesse or subtle sarcasm would have been entirely wasted, and so incensed had he been over the uncouth jeers of the sheriff, that he could not refrain from talking to him in a language he could understand.

But one thing the sheriff had accomplished —he had succeeded in enlisting on Stephen Hamilton's behalf the most efficient human sleuth-hound that the science of criminology had ever produced.

When the sheriff had placed his prisoner in one of the canoes and had charged one of the St. Pierre lads to guard him, he returned to the house, and, assisted by Louis and Pierre, had the body conveyed to another canoe.

Dr. Taylor, incensed though he might be, was nevertheless forced to assist, for it was quite true that he was coroner for the county, and, no matter what his private opinion might be, he must obey the law as represented just then by the sheriff.

When that had been done, the sheriff harangued the four men who were in Hamilton's employ, warning them to hold themselves in readiness to come into Plaster Rock for the inquest.

With that he stumped off to the canoe, and when Dr. Taylor had expressed his deep regret, he followed and climbed into the second canoe, where the body of the murdered man had been placed.

It was a mournful sight to see the two craft slip away, with the murdered man in one, and his suspected murderer in the other.

Neither Blake nor Tinker moved until both canoes had disappeared from view behind a jutting point. Then Tinker said:

"You said something when you called that sheriff an ivory headed dumb-bell, guv'nor! He is that, and likewise a gink, a boob, and a yahoo! What are you going to do now?"

Blake lighted a cigarette.

"Yes, as the papers say, a thoroughly enjoyable time was had by all, Tinker. Quite a pleasant little visit, take it all in all. A charming gentleman, our friend the sheriff.

"But that doesn't help us any. The thing we have got to discover is how that wireless outfit came to be in Hamilton's box.

"There is no question but that it was a plant. But who placed it there? When was it done? That is the problem we have got to solve and solve quickly if we are to save Hamilton from damaging publicity."

"What about the Jap, guv'nor?" asked Tinker in a low tone

"That is exactly what I am asking myself," answered Blake. "I am also asking myself what about Ralph Sweeney, my lad.

"I can't quite dismiss that man from my mind. But we cannot go ahead there until we have heard from Lindsay.

"His telegram may give us a lead. As for the Jap—we shall keep a very close eye on him. If I could only fathom what he was at last night, it would help up, I believe. I am sure it had some connection with the crime.

THE EIGHTH CHAPTER.   A Little Deduction— Sweeney's Shady Past— "It Looks Bad for Hamilton!" — Kamoto Disappears.

FOR all the visible effort Sexton Blake seemed to make during the rest of that day, one might have been excused for thinking that he was doing very little to dig up evidence which would help to clear Stephen Hamilton of the terrible crime with which he was charged.

But when Blake seemed most detached from a thing was usually when his mind was working at highest pressure, and the present was no exception.

One thing had so far not come to light; that was the fact that Stephen Hamilton had in his safe a large sum of money which had been the property of the dead man.

Blake believed Hamilton implicitly in his statement that he had paid that money to Carson, and, after destroying the promissory note which Carson had handed back to him, had put the money in the safe at Carson's request.

But Blake knew full well that if the sheriff could but get his teeth into that extra evidence, so to say, he would worry it to pieces, and then put it together again in the form of additional damning evidence against Hamilton.

It would take very delicate handling to steer round that rock, and Blake knew it.

Two or three lines of action had already suggested themselves, but for the moment he was determined to play a waiting game.

Firstly, he wanted to see what Lindsay had to say; and secondly, he was on the watch for some break in the defences of the unknown murderer.

That this person had been, and still was, in the neighbourhood, Blake felt sure.

He did not believe that the murderer who had carried out his crime with such elaborate pains would depart altogether from the scene of his crime until he had seen just what the result was to be.

Moreover, the planting of the wireless set in Hamilton's box strengthened that theory. If Blake could only orient the time of that action, he knew he would be a long way ahead in his attempt to solve the mystery.

He felt pretty sure that the wireless apparatus had not been planted in Hamilton's trunk before the crime, for the risk of discovery by the intended victim would have been too great.

Then it must be assumed that the apparatus had been placed there after the murder had been carried out. When could that have been accomplished?

Shortly after the murder, Stephen Hamilton had hastened into Plaster Rock and on to Aroostook Junction. He had been away from the camp all that afternoon and evening as well as during the night.

Since then there would have been very little chance for anyone to open up the trunk and place the apparatus in it. There had been too many persons about for that. Therefore, it must have been while Hamilton was in Plaster Rock, Blake reasoned.

That brought him to a certain extent to a point where be could make a logical guess at the period of time.

Next, who was there at the camp during that time? There had been the two French Canadian guides and the cook. There had also been the valet.

And on their return from Plaster Rock they had also found Ralph Sweeney on the veranda. By his own words, he had confessed to having entered the room where the murdered man lay. Had he also entered Hamilton's room?

Blake hadn't the slightest doubt that Kamoto could answer that question.

On the other hand, he considered it would be unwise to interrogate the Jap while the issue was so beclouded. If the Jap had been mixed up in the affair in conjunction with another, then the question would only meet with a blank denial, and, further, would cause Kamoto to warn Sweeney, if Sweeney had also been mixed up in it.

It was most puzzling. Blake certainly entertained suspicions against Sweeney. He also was intrigued as to what part the Jap had played.

Had the two been working in collusion? Had Ralph Sweeney planned the murder, and had he carried it out with the assistance of Kamoto? Or was Sweeney quite innocent and had the Jap conceived and carried out the crime alone?

Or, alternatively, was the Jap innocent and was it the work of Sweeney, either alone or in conjunction with some other person or persons at present unknown?

It all resolved itself into a vicious circle, the exact meaning of which Blake could not yet solve.

So many factors had to be taken into account. For instance, there were the shots which had been fired at Tinker's canoe when he and young St. Pierre were on their way back from Plaster Rock.

Sweeney had confessed to being responsible, and had claimed that he and his guide had been night-hunting and mistaken the canoe for a swimming moose.

Sweeney might successfully maintain that, but it was difficult to credit the guide with such a mistake. Any self-respecting woodsman would be ashamed to own to it.

From Louis and Pierre, Blake had gathered that Sweeney's guide was a "bad egg," and young St. Pierre had told Tinker the same thing. But if the shots had been deliberate why had they been fired?

Did Sweeney know from his guide that a canoe had left the camp for Plaster Rock soon after he had departed for his own camp? Did he know in some way that either he or Tinker, or both of them, were in the canoe?

Had he, through a guilty conscience, feared that Sexton Blake was making some move to discover the person or persons who had killed Angus Carson?

If Ralph Sweeney were guilty, then he would never be fool enough to discount the danger to be feared from Sexton Blake, as the sheriff had swept aside the value of Blake's methods.

Sweeney was too much man of the world to make that mistake. Then, if that were so, was the shooting a deliberate attempt to remove Blake and his assistant from the scene—that is, presuming that he thought the canoe was occupied by the pair?

It would not entail much risk, for while he would certainly be strongly reprimanded for night-shooting, he would never be convicted on what would be accepted by any jury as a pure accident. There was certainly food for thought in that incident which had befallen Tinker.

He was still in an uncommunicative mood by the time dinner, or, rather, supper was served. Kamoto waited on the table as impassively as if no such thing as a crime had taken place at the camp.

In his imperturbability he was well matched by Sexton Blake, and, watching the two of them, Tinker could not help but wonder just what secret process of thought was going on behind the vacant-looking moon face of the Oriental and the cold, chiselled mask of the

European.

They had just finished the meal, and were sitting smoking on the veranda while Kamoto cleared away the things, when the sound of voices reached them, and through the gloom they made out a figure at the edge of the water.

It came towards them a few seconds later, and when it was within the penumbra of the big table-lamp they recognised one of Napoleon St, Pierre's numerous offspring.

"Telegram, m'sieu," he said. "M'sieu perhaps will send wan reply?"

Blake thanked him as he took the envelope.

"You might wait, and I will let you know," he said. Then he tore open the flap and took out the folded form.

As he had suspected, it was from Lindsay, and although in private code, so familiar was Blake with the code that he read its meaning almost as quickly as if I had been written in plain English. It ran as follows:

"Man inquired about well known here. Financier and promoter on big scale. Been mixed up in several big deals, some of which of rather shady nature. Only association can trace with Carson is in connection with attempt to get control of Northern Wireless Corporation. Was beaten by Carson all along the line and dropped very large amount.

"Confidential inquiries show that has been making another attempt to get control, and in some way managed to secure option on several large blocks of shares. Carson also after same shares.

"Is very shrewd and cunning and absolutely ruthless. If mixed up in any business with him suggest you watch him very carefully. Quite capable of any action to gain his own ends.

" LINDSAY."

Blake carefully folded up the paper before he glanced towards the lad who had brought it.

"No; there will be no reply to take back," he said. "Are you returning to night, or will you have some supper and sleep here?"

"Merci, m'sieu! I sink I mak' for 'ome to-night."

Blake rose and walked to the edge of the veranda.

"Very well!" he said carelessly. "We will give you a hand with your canoe. Come along. Tinker!"

Wondering a little, Tinker rose and accompanied Blake down to the edge of the lake. But as they went along he discovered why Blake had offered to assist the young fellow to launch the canoe which he was perfectly capable of launching alone.

"Do you think you can trust this young fellow, Tinker?" he asked, in a low tone.

"Quite sure', guv'nor! He is on the level all right."

"Then tell him to paddle along this side of the lake until he is well out of hearing of the camp. Tell him to pull his canoe up there and wait for us.

"We may be a long time, or we may come soon, but I want to make a little expedition to-night, and I don't want the hands here at the camp to know what we are up to."

Tinker bent over the canoe and held a short colloquy with the young fellow. Then the canoe went darting away, and was lost in the gloom almost before the echoes of their "Good-nights!" had died away.

"He will wait on the other side of the first point," whispered Tinker.

"Good! I think— Hallo! What is this, Tinker?"

Blake had come to a stop, and was gazing out over the lake. Tinker peered into the darkness, and was able to make out a dim shape approaching the shore.

It grounded gently, and the next moment a burly figure came towards them.

"Sweeney!" muttered Blake, in an undertone. "Now, what the dickens does he want here?"

It was Ralph Sweeney and none other, and as he paused before them he said:

"Is that you, Mr. Hamilton?"

"No," answered Blake; "Mr. Hamilton is not here. It is Mr. Sweeney, isn't it?"

"Yes. I paddled over again to see what had been discovered about the accident. I should like to be of assistance, if I could. Ah, I see now it is you, Mr. Blake!"

"Yes. I am afraid there is nothing you can do, Mr. Sweeney. My assistant and I are the only ones at the camp. Mr. Carson's body was taken into Plaster Rock this afternoon by the sheriff."

"Oh, he turned up, did he? What did he say, Mr. Blake? Does he agree with your theory that it was a crime?"

"Apparently he did," responded Blake, in level terms. "He felt so sure that he immediately arrested Stephen Hamilton on suspicion, and claims he has indisputable proof of his guilt.

"And I must confess that the evidence is certainly very strong against Hamilton. It has, naturally, been a great shock to me!"

"Good heavens! Hamilton arrested!" exclaimed Sweeney. "How on earth is he supposed to have killed Carson?"

"By a very ingenious method," said Blake. "It seems that a rifle was discovered attached to one of the branches of a fir-tree in that grove over there. It had a small wireless receiving apparatus attached to the stock, and this, in turn, was connected with the trigger.

"Investigation showed that it was trained exactly on the spot where Angus Carson would sit when at meals, and the theory is that the wave which caused the trap to act was sent by Hamilton when he went into the living-room to get the box of cigars.

"It looks pretty bad for Hamilton, as part of a wireless sending apparatus was found in one of his trunks."

"I can scarcely credit it!" ejaculated Sweeney. "I am most deeply pained at the news. If I can be of any assistance, I hope you will allow me to help. Carson was an old friend of mine, and I am naturally keen that his murderer should be run to earth.

"But Stephen Hamilton! It doesn't seem possible! What motive could he have?"

"As far as can be discovered, there was a very big financial transaction between him and Carson. As a matter of fact, he has confessed that a big sum of money in his safe had really been paid by him to Carson to redeem a promissory-note.

"The transaction took place just the day before Carson was killed. Yes," sighed, Blake, "it certainly looks bad for Hamilton."

There was a brief silence. It was plain that Sweeney was waiting for an invitation to go up on the veranda; but Blake was determined that he should be given no opportunity of communicating with the Jap even by signals. At last Sweeney laughed harshly.

"Well, if Hamilton did it, I hope he gets the rope!" he said. "I'll be at the inquest to watch what takes place. Do you know when it will be?"

"Either to-morrow or next day. You could find out at Black Water."

"I'll do that. Many thanks, Mr. Blake. Will you be staying on for any length of time?"

"No. I am very upset over what has happened here. I shall leave in a day or two."

"Well, I hope we meet again under more pleasant circumstances. —By the way, I nearly shot your young friend last night, I am afraid it was very careless of me. I am awfully sorry, and I don't blame him for getting ratty with me."

"I think he has forgotten it," drawled Blake. "Only it is a risky business to go night hunting with canoes about."

"Quite so. I shall take good care to avoid it in future. Well, good-night! I will be getting back."

With that Sweeney made for his canoe, and a few seconds later it disappeared in the gloom.

"You certainly will be at that inquest, if I have anything to say about it!" murmured Blake, as he turned to go back to the house. "Got what I was waiting for my lad, and Ralph Sweeney gave it to me.

"We shall certainly need that canoe of St. Pierre's to night. And now to get the men away to the bunk-shack so we can make an early start. I'll tell Kamoto he needn't worry to remain up any longer."

Tinker remained on the veranda while Blake entered the house to give instructions to the Jap.

He was not there, however, so Blake passed out by the back, and made for the bunk shack. As he entered it he saw the three French Canadians sitting at the table playing cards.

"Where is Kamoto?" asked Blake.

Louis glanced up.

"Me, I not know, m'sieu. Kamoto tak his box and go off into ze woods."

"The three of you turn out and find him!" ordered Blake. "Tell him I want to speak with him before he turns in."

He returned to the veranda while the two guides and the cook took lanterns and went off to find the Jap.

But at the end of half an hour, when the three French Canadians came back to say that they had searched far and wide but could find no sign of the Jap, Blake suddenly glanced towards Tinker.

Each knew what the other was thinking. That thought was that Kamoto had gone for good.

Peering through the window, Blake and Tinker saw Sweeney seated at a rough pine table on which was a decanter of whisky and a couple of glasses. On the other side stood the guide, leaning forward regarding Sweeney with a leer of triumph. (*Chapter 9.*)

THE NINTH CHAPTER.   Closing the Net —A Night Expedition —Attempted Blackmail —And the Result —The Jap Turns Up— A Triple Tragedy.

BLAKE knew that it was utterly useless to attempt to count on what Kamoto might be up to as a factor affecting his own intentions.

One thing loomed up that must be regarded as a possibility to be taken into account, and that was the chance that the Jap had gone for good.

Blake was chagrined that his plans should have been upset by such an occurrence. He had counted on having Kamoto just where he wanted him when he might choose to act.

He had looked for and had hoped for some action on the part of one of the suspects which might give him a lead, and had found that in the visit Ralph Sweeney had paid to the camp that evening.

But he did not desire the initiative taken by both the suspects. That was just where Kamoto had upset his plans.

Moreover, he liked it even less that it had followed so soon on the heels of Sweeney's visit. Had Kamoto received some signal from Sweeney while the latter had been talking to Blake and Tinker?

Blake and the lad discussed that possibility in all its phases, but, canvass each moment as they might, they could not recall a single suspicious moment when Sweeney might have conveyed some message to the Jap, even though they might have a subtle and secret code between them.

On the other hand, while the Oriental had appeared completely unmoved by the arrest of Stephen Hamilton, it may have been that the questioning he had undergone at the hands of the sheriff and Hamilton's arrest had made him fear that his own admissions might lead to his arrest at any moment, and he had decided to "go while the going was good."

But, whatever the reason, Blake knew that even on the chance of it upsetting his plans for that night, he must go ahead just the same, if he were to fulfil the vow to Stephen Hamilton.

He and Tinker sat on the veranda until long past eleven. Blake would have wished to start sooner, but he was hoping against hope that the Jap would return.

But when midnight drew on and there was no sign of the valet, he gave the signal to go.

While Tinker went round to the back to make sure that the three French Canadians were in bed and asleep, Blake blew out the lamp and made his way slowly across to the edge of the lake.

He waited there for Tinker to join him, and when the lad had done so, they began walking along the sand towards the point behind which young St. Pierre should be waiting for them.

Blake's object was a very definite one. His reception of Ralph Sweeney, his apparent acceptance of Hamilton's guilt, and his other statements to Sweeney had all been for a carefully calculated effect.

His suspicions that Sweeney was the moving spirit in the murder of Angus Carson were very strong, but he had realised even when those suspicions first came to him, that it would be necessary for him to go very carefully if he were to succeed in trapping the murderer.

Sweeney was no fool, and Blake had seen enough of him to know that he would be quite untroubled by conscience after his ghastly crime.

That fact would keep him on his guard, but, on the other hand, Blake had counted on Sweeney doing just what he had done that evening—coming to the Hamilton camp to find out what developments had taken place.

He would know, through his guide, that the sheriff had come, and it was altogether likely as well that from the same source he knew all about Hamilton's arrest before he put in an appearance.

More than that, Lindsay's telegram not only revealed that Sweeney had sufficient knowledge of wireless science to evolve a subtle scheme of murder such as Angus Carson had been the victim of, but also it provided motive which until then had been absolutely lacking.

His anxiety to impress Blake with the fact that he and Carson had been friends did not tally very well with what Lindsay had to say, and Blake knew that Lindsay was absolutely reliable.

Therefore, while he felt convinced in his own mind that when he had succeeded in unmasking Ralph Sweeney he would have unmasked the murderer, he had also been anxious to spring his trap at a time when he knew exactly where the Jap was and what he was up to.

Of the latter he was still in doubt. He felt certain that Kamoto was being influenced, in some way by his master's murder, but just how he could not make out. He had counted on clearing up that question when he had finished with Ralph Sweeney.

He did not know how soon the riddle was to be answered.

They found the young French-Canadian asleep on the sand beside his canoe. When they had woke him, Blake asked him if he thought he could paddle across to Sweeney's camp and land them near it without discovery.

The lad assured him that he could; so, when the canoe had been pushed into the water, Tinker took the bow paddle while St. Pierre took the stern.

Blake sat in the middle, leaving it to the two young fellows to do the work, for he knew that Tinker could paddle almost as noiselessly as the woodsman.

For the first part of the journey they paddled at a strong, steady pace, but when they were half-way across the lake they eased the stroke, and dipped the blades with infinite caution.

Not a word was spoken, not even a whisper, for over the water at night the smallest sounds travel with extraordinary clearness.

They were perhaps half a mile or so from the opposite shore when Blake, who was peering ahead, caught the faint gleam of a light. In silence he turned and pointed with his hand. Young St. Pierre nodded, and brought the nose of the canoe round the veriest trifle.

It was evident that someone was still up at the Sweeney camp, or else Sweeney slept with a light burning.

The canoe grounded about two hundred yards south of the camp, and leaving young St. Pierre in charge, Blake and Tinker shifted their pistols into a convenient position for quick action, and started towards the camp.

There was plenty of cover, for Sweeney had not cleared away as much ground as had Hamilton, and the fir and spruce belt ran almost up to the camp. As they drew near the edge they again caught the gleam of a light, and when they had reconnoitred a little, they judged it came from the room which would be the living-room.

"I am going across," whispered Blake. "Follow me, Tinker, and don't make a noise. If Sweeney's asleep, I am going inside. If not, then I shall decide afterwards what to do."

Without waiting for Tinker's reply, he dropped to his knees, and started across towards the house.

Tinker followed him a few seconds later, and saw that Blake was making for an open window which gave on to the veranda on the side of the house which faced them, and through which came the gleam of light.

He was close at Blake's heels when the latter crawled up on to the veranda, and as Tinker followed and crouched beside his master, he felt a touch on his arm enjoining silence. At the same moment he heard the sound of voices in the room beyond.

"You don't know who you are dealing with," came in tones which they both recognised as Sweeney's, although they were thick and slurring in accent, proving that he had been drinking.

"No man ever held me up yet and got away with it. You agreed to do a certain thing for a certain price. You did the job, and you got paid. That ends it as far as I am concerned."

As he finished speaking another voice sounded, and from the fact that the words used were those of the habitant, it was a pretty good bet that it was Sweeney's guide.

"All zat ees true, m'sieu, but you—you know not me. I tol' you zat I would do ze work. I did ze work, and you, m'sieu, you pay. But zat ees not enough.

"Me, Gaspard, I want ten tousan' dollars. Zen I go far 'way. I go to ze United States, an' I not com' bak nevaire. Zat is wat I say."

"You were paid five thousand dollars to do nothing more than sit in your canoe and flash a mirror across the lake!" snarled Sweeney.

"Now you have the nerve to ask for ten thousand more. I say you will get not another cent. That is final. So what about it?"

"Wat about eet?" exclaimed the guide. "You ask me wat about eet, m'sieu! I tell you wat about eet. Me, I see wat ze shereef sink about eet. He lak ver' mooch hav' you w'ere he now got M'sieu Hamilton."

"Shut up, you fool!" broke in Sweeney. "If you think you can threaten me, you are barking up the wrong tree. Why, you scum of the lumber camps, I will shoot you as I would a dog!"

"You sink so? You leesten to me, m'sieu! I, Gaspard, fear you not. You gif to me ten tousan' dollars, or I wheesper wan leetle word in ze ear of M'sieu Shereef."

There was a short silence, during which both Blake and Tinker lifted their heads and risked a cautious peep into the room.

To Sexton Blake had come with dramatic force full confirmation of his suspicions. In those few seconds he had secured proof of far more than he had dared hope for.

He knew now beyond the shadow or a doubt that Ralph Sweeney was the murderer of Angus Carson; and he knew, further, exactly how Sweeney had known the psychological moment to spring his devilish trap.

In quarrelling over the blood-money, the two rogues had delivered themselves into the hands of Sexton Blake.

Peering over the edge, they saw Sweeney seated at a rough pine table, on which stood a bottle of whisky and a jug of water. On the other side of the table stood the guide, and at the moment he was leaning forward regarding Sweeney with a leer of triumph.

But Ralph Sweeney had spoken only too truly when he said that it was a dangerous game to try and hold him up.

If the guide had been able to read character as well as Sexton Blake, he would have realised that the cold blue eyes that were regarding him from beneath half-closed lids mirrored a soul capable of anything.

Sober, Sweeney was ruthless enough. Drunk, as he was now, he was about ten times more dangerous than a nest of rattlesnakes; and Sexton Blake knew it.

Suddenly Sweeney laughed. His lids lifted, and he bent forward, his eyes fixed on his vis-a-vis.

Something of the menace of those hard blue orbs seemed to penetrate the mind of the guide, for he shifted and started to rise. Again Sweeney laughed, and the next moment he had jerked out a heavy revolver.

"Sit down!" he snarled. "Don't spoil my aim by getting up. So you would blackmail me, would you? I'll pay you, and in good heavy coin, you scum!"

"M'sieu," began the guide, in a tone or frantic fear.

Crash!

The revolver spoke just once, and as the bullet crashed full between the eyes of the wretched man, Blake and Tinker saw him throw up his arms and slump to the floor.

"You'll collect payment at the bottom of the lake," rasped Sweeney, as he got to his feet and stood regarding his victim. "Blackmail Ralph Sweeney, will you? When I start out—"

Ralph Sweeney never finished that boast. Even as his lips were framing the next word something flashed at the other side of the room.

From behind the door a figure glided, and before Sweeney was aware of his danger, before Sexton Blake or Tinker could call out a warning, Kamoto hurled himself upon the murderer.

There came the flash of a knife; then Ralph Sweeney staggered back, with a great crimson gash showing in his throat. He coughed once, twice. Then crashed to the floor.

"My heavens! What a rough-house," rapped Blake. "Come on. Tinker, we must get Kamoto!"

Even as he spoke Blake was pushing the window higher so that they might crawl through. At the sound the Jap turned.

Then they saw him bend himself over. Blake cried out. The Jap bent still lower and then, even as Blake's hands reached his shoulders, he crashed forward. He had committed hari-kari.

"DO you not intend to put Mr. Blake on the witness-stand, sheriff?"

Dr. Taylor, coroner at the inquest on the body of Angus Carson, asked the question with a hint of surprise in his tone.

At the back of the little office in the hotel at Plaster Rock, Sexton Blake and Tinker were sitting among the lumber men who had come from far and wide to listen to the proceedings.

Behind Dr. Taylor sat the jury, made up of the storekeeper, the clerk, the railway agent, and the rest lumbermen.

The proceedings had gone ahead rapidly under the direction of the sheriff, who had placed his witnesses on the stand in quick succession. It was little wonder that Dr. Taylor was surprised that he did not intend to take Blake's evidence, for he did not think the sheriff would drag his expressed contempt of Blake and his methods into the official examination.

But it appeared that was just what he intended doing, for in reply to the question he snapped:

"We have already examined the three witnesses who were at the camp when the murder was committed. The other witness can tell us nuthin' of any value. He was not there at the time. All he knows is what the prisoner told him. I am ready now fer the verdict of the jury."

Blake rose.

"You will please excuse me, Mr. Coroner, but despite what Sheriff Maxwell says. I have very strong reasons for wishing to give evidence.

"As the case now stands, that is from the evidence given, the jury have practically been charged to bring a verdict of murder against an innocent man.

"As I am in possession of absolute proof that he is innocent, then, I think, in the cause of justice, my evidence had better be heard before these proceedings degenerate into a farce."

"I object tu the jury bein' filled with crazy the'ries!" protested the sheriff. "The case is clean open and shut!"

Blake whirled on him.

"You are quite right in that, and that is the only thing about this case you are right in," he snapped. "The less you say the better. You will have less to retract afterwards.

"I am a British subject, and as such I demand that my evidence be heard. Mr. Coroner, have I your permission?"

"Certainly, Mr. Blake. I shall be very glad to hear your evidence."

Blake stepped to the little table that did duty as a witness-stand and took the oath. Then turning to Dr. Taylor he said:

"I do not propose going into unnecessary detail, Mr. Coroner, but I shall be as brief as possible. But first I must inform you that another inquest will be necessary, and this time it will be upon three bodies instead of one.

"Those three bodies are at present lying in Ralph Sweeney's camp; and the death of all three is directly due to the murder of Angus Carson."

There was a general muttering of excitement among the lumbermen, and all hands shifted to listen better.

"I have complete proof of each statement I shall make," went on Blake. "To begin with, it is an accepted fact that Angus Carson was killed by the rifle which has been exhibited here to-day, and it is further admitted that it was probably discharged by a wireless wave as was originally suggested by me.

"But it is not a fact that Stephen Hamilton was the man who put that fatal wireless wave into motion.

"The murder-plot was conceived and carried out by Ralph Sweeney, who has, or rather had, a camp on the opposite side of the lake.

"I was puzzled for a long time as to how he could have known the exact moment to act, but now I know.

"If you will recall the original statement made by Mr. Hamilton, Mr. Coroner, you will remember that he spoke of seeing a canoe near the upper end of the lake shortly after the murder.

"That, he stated, was the only sign of anyone they could see, and, owing to the great distance, the man in that canoe was not suspected of having had anything to do with the murder."

"That was an incorrect assumption, the man in that canoe was Ralph Sweeney's French Canadian guide, who, I believe, bore an unenviable reputation.

"He came near enough to Hamilton's camp to watch the movements of those on the veranda, probably through a telescope. That is purely a hypothesis on my part, but from the guide's own lips I know that he signalled across the lake to Sweeney by means of flashing a mirror.

"On seeing the flash, Sweeney, who was in his own camp at the time, brought his wireless-sending apparatus into action, with the result that the receiving apparatus which was attached to the rifle before you brought the rifle into play. You know how successful the attempt was.

"I suspected Sweeney from the first, and also I should say I was very puzzled as to what part the Jap servant, Kamoto, had played.

"When the wireless apparatus was discovered in Mr. Hamilton's box, I knew that it could only be a plant with the intention of throwing suspicion on Mr. Hamilton.

"I was quite willing that the sheriff should act on this, for it gave me a free hand to follow up the clues I already had.

"I felt positive that either the Jap or Sweeney had placed the box there; and it wasn't very difficult to place the time as being when Stephen Hamilton had come into Plaster Rock to report the murder.

"I worked on that theory, but must confess that my plans were upset by the mysterious disappearance from the camp last night of the Jap.

"However, with the aid of my assistant and one of Napoleon St. Pierre's sons, I crossed the lake about midnight last night. My assistant and I found that Sweeney was in the living-room of the camp in conversation with his guide.

"They were in the midst of an altercation. It appears that Sweeney had paid the guide five thousand dollars for his share in the affair, but the guide was holding out for a further ten thousand.

"He promised, if he received this, to go to the United States and not return. During that altercation Ralph Sweeney confessed to the murder of Angus Carson.

"The guide, however, little realised the type of man he had to deal with," went on Blake. "He persisted in his threats, and, even as we watched, Sweeney drew his pistol and shot the guide. Death was instantaneous.

"Immediately after, while Sweeney was apostrophising the dead man, a third factor appeared in the form of Kamoto.

"Both my assistant and myself tried to call out to Sweeney, but before we could do so, the Jap had sprung upon him and had plunged a knife into his throat. It was a mortal thrust, and Sweeney died almost at once. We managed to get the window open, but before we could reach the Jap, he had committed hari-kari; and thus we had a triple tragedy to deal with.

"It is quite plain, Mr. Coroner, that the Japanese servant suspected Sweeney, and in some way managed to confirm his suspicions. Then he left the camp to carry out his terrible vengeance.

"It seems most probable that he was very much attached to his dead master, and determined to avenge his death.

"Later on, I shall be glad to put all these facts into a written statement. But in view of the fact that Ralph Sweeney was the murderer of Angus Carson, and that Sweeney is dead, no one can be held for the crime. Therefore. I demand the immediate release of Mr. Hamilton.

"I think it is obvious that the sheriff has been allowed to blunder long enough, and I suggest that, instead of wasting his time here trying to blacken the name of a very honourable gentleman, he would be better employed attending to his duty at Sweeney's camp."

There was what Tinker termed "some shemozzle" among the lumbermen when Blake had finished his evidence.

They hazed the sheriff in the most unmerciful manner, nor did they let up until that very much sadder, though possibly not wiser, man had departed for Black Water on his way to Sweeney's camp. He made no attempt to apologise to Blake, nor did the latter desire him to do so.

Blake had had more than satisfaction as his evidence had dripped coldly and ruthlessly on the hearing of those present at the inquest.

And if the sheriff had needed confirmation of the nightmare that had crept upon him, he found it in plenty in the shambles at Ralph Sweeney's camp.

Following the inquest, Blake, Tinker and Stephen Hamilton returned to the camp, and in the crisp days in the big woods wiped from their minds the ugly phases of the affair, although their pleasure was tempered by the sad tragedy which had removed the genial and lovable old man from their midst.

They saw nothing more of the sheriff, although rumours reached them that, while the whole countryside was rocking with laughter over his discomfiture, the hilarity was suppressed when the victim was about, for he was plunging about the woods like a maddened grizzly.

Probably no one was more delighted over Blake's triumph than Dr. Taylor, whose official position had made things so distasteful and so difficult.

As for Blake himself, he just smiled that enigmatic smile of his, and no one knew exactly what he was thinking about the whole affair.

THE END.
[27000 WORDS]